Marie Alker Günther

Tales And Legends Of The Tyrol

Marie Alker Günther

Tales And Legends Of The Tyrol

ISBN/EAN: 9783741149337

Manufactured in Europe, USA, Canada, Australia, Japa

Cover: Foto ©Andreas Hilbeck / pixelio.de

Manufactured and distributed by brebook publishing software
(www.brebook.com)

Marie Alker Günther

Tales And Legends Of The Tyrol

TALES AND LEGENDS

OF THE

TYROL.

COLLECTED AND ARRANGED

BY

MADAME LA COMTESSE A. VON GÜNTHER.

LONDON:

CHAPMAN AND HALL, 193, PICCADILLY.

1874.

PRINTED BY TAYLOR AND CO.,
LITTLE QUEEN STREET, LINCOLN'S INN FIELDS

DEDICATION.

———◆———

To those who dare the unfrequented mountain paths and passes of the Tyrol, in search of all that is wonderful and grand, this work is respectfully dedicated by

THE AUTHORESS.

PREFACE.

THE Tyrol, the land of glory and tradition, the wonder-garden of the world, so often visited but so little known, forms the theme of the following volume; and in dedicating it to the public the authoress feels certain of a fair share of their approval, perhaps, even, of their thanks; for many are the dangers which have been incurred in its production, and many are the days of weary walks and severe trials that it has cost.

There are no railroads in the mountains, and even cart-tracks are "few and far between," and those who wish to see the almost hidden beauty, must, in passing through this enchanted land, undergo all the authoress has undergone, and share with her the pleasure as well as the pain.

All that is grand and beautiful, all that is gorgeous and sublime, all that is shocking and terrible, is to be met with at every step in the Tyrol ; and the following legends are but a poor illustration of the old proverb, "There are finer fish in the sea than ever came out of it."

The strange dialect of the inhabitants of this curious country, renders it almost impossible for any foreigner unacquainted with their language to understand what they would so willingly recount ; and, in consequence, thousands and thousands of sight-seers yearly pass through, perfectly at a loss how to gratify their curiosity, except in the natural grandeur and beauty of the mountain world. The authoress has often noticed large parties of English and foreign visitors wandering aimlessly through a valley, round a ruin, or on the borders of a lake, whose history they have vainly tried to discover; for however willing the poor honest peasants are to explain all their visitors would wish to know, yet their kindly efforts are of course unavailing, and these foreigners go away back to their own countries, having passed over, and perhaps seen *all*, without knowing anything.

This little work, then, written first for the pleasure of its authoress, she now places in the hands of the public, trusting that it may not only be a useful guide, but a pleasant com-

panion in the mountains in which it took its
origin.

How lovely the land of those beauties unseen,
   Which touch on the borders of Nature's fair soul!
How bright are those landscapes, so soft and serene,
   Which kiss the sweet homesteads of my own dear Tyrol!

MARY COUNTESS A. VON GÜNTHER.

INDEX.

—◆—

Index.

TALES AND LEGENDS

OF

THE TYROL.

———◆———

THE GIANT JORDAN.

To the east of the Ungarkopf, and high above the cavern called Eggerskeller, there stands, close to a dizzy chasm in the rocks, the Kohlhütte (coal hut), which is surrounded by steep grey mountain walls. Not long since there resided in this hut a wild man, with his wife Fangga. Jordan, for this was the name of the giant, employed himself in stealing children and beasts which he devoured, and he occupied his time also in hunting the poor fairies, whom he caught and killed, or shut up in underground prisons.

One day he brought home a fairy, most probably

B

one of those which resided in the Eggerskeller, and
who was already more dead than alive. He threw
her down at the feet of his wife, and was on the
point of killing her, but Fangga said, "Let the
thing live; it will be of use to me."

"So," growled the monster; "what can you do
with her?"

"I should like to have her in the hut to make
her work," answered his gigantic wife.

"Take then the thing," shouted the giant; "the
white cat to the black one!" for the giant couple
had in their hut a huge black cat which the giant
had made a present to his wife in a similar manner
after having caught it in the mountains.

The poor fairy now bore the yoke of servitude,
under the giant couple, who called her Hitte Hatte.
She was obliged to wear servant's clothes and do
servant's drudgery, which she did so cleverly and
quickly that Fangga was contented with her, and
treated her as kindly as it was in her brutal nature
to do. Hitte Hatte was kind to the cat, fed her
regularly, let her sleep in her own bed, and got
altogether fond of her. Although she had now
taken entirely the nature of a human being, she

constantly longed to be free of the giants, and one day she took the occasion while Jordan was out and Fangga sleeping, to slip down into the valley and to seek her fortune amongst mankind. The cat, as though she knew the intention of her friend, followed her every step of the way, and so it happened that one evening a pretty girl, followed by a huge black cat, entered the farm (of Seehaus, which is close to the village of Strad, in the Gurgl valley,) and offered her services. The farm people, whose name was Krapf, a very good and worthy couple, were not very well off just then, as they had suffered some heavy losses, and therefore at that time did not keep many servants. So they engaged the pretty girl for very small wages, without even asking her who she was or from whence she came. She did her work joyfully and well, (and with her blessings entered Seehaus ;) it was a pleasure to see how beautifully Hitte Hatte, for this name she had kept up, managed and arranged everything. The cleverest old peasant woman would never have been able to do so well as she did. She went about her work quietly, spoke little, and never anything without purpose ; was always modest and reserved, and the people of the farm left her to go on in her quiet way just as she liked.) Her greatest pet was and remained the cat, which was also very useful in keeping the house and buildings clear of rats and mice. Hitte Hatte only knew one fear, and that was the giant, who on account of her flight had made a most fearful noise, and beaten his wife without mercy; but in the valley he could not touch her, for the village boundaries were every year blessed by the priest, and there were all round about little crosses and chapels, of which the gigantic race of pagans had the greatest terror.

While Hitte Hatte was still in Seehaus Farm, two boys of Strad had climbed up the Ungarkopf to gather strawberries, and approached by accident the giant's abode. As the evening shadows began to fall the boys got tired and hungry, and were about to return home, when they saw blue smoke arising quite close to them, which ascended out of Jordan's Kohlhütte, and one of the boys shouted to the other, "Look at the smoke! there, I am sure they are making cakes; let us go and see if we can't get some."

They soon arrived at the door of the hut, which

was carefully closed, so one of them scrambled up on the roof, removed one of the wooden tiles and peeped down below. Fangga, who was busy at her kitchen, heard him in a moment, and called out, "Who is up there on my roof?"

The boy answered, "It is I with my good companion. We are hungry, and pray you kindly to give us something to eat."

Fangga opened the door and called out, "Come in, my boys, and you shall have something, but be quick and creep into this hole (she pointed out the stove), and keep very quiet there, for the 'wild man' is coming very soon, and if he catches sight of you he will eat you bones and all."

On hearing this the boys were terrified out of their wits, and crept into the stove, and directly afterwards the giant entered the hut, and sniffing round with hideous rolling eyes, he shouted to his wife, "I smell, I smell human meat!"

But Fangga, who had not been educated in any Innsbruck school, answered him very sharply, "You smell, you smell the devil!"

Then the giant gave such a tremendous snort that the whole hut trembled as though it had been

shaken by the wind, and the boys terrified lest the
stove should fall and kill them, jumped out of it.
As Jordan caught sight of them his rage grew still
more horrible; he overloaded Fangga with imprecations and abuse, shut the boys up in a cupboard
and took the keys with him while he ran off to catch
a lost goat of whose bell he just caught the sound.
The poor boys now began to scream and implore,
and at last Fangga, cruel and hard as she was, was
touched with pity, and consented to release them.
But as she had not the key of the [cupboard, she
kicked at the door till it flew open, let the boys out,
and told them the best means of making their
escape, and away they went as fast as ever their legs
would carry them.

They had not gone long when the wild man returned home, but without his goat, which had also escaped him, so he vowed now to kill the boys; but as
the cupboard was empty and he could nowhere find
them, he thundered new imprecations at Fangga,
who however took no notice of them. The savage
monster then seized his boarskin mantle, and set off
in pursuit of them. He arrived at last on the edge
of a wild roaring mountain-torrent, on the other

side of which he caught sight of them, and he called out in the sweetest and softest voice he could command, "Tell me, dear boys, how you got over the river!"

"Ho! wild man," shouted the boys, "go up the river, and further on you will find the plank over which we crossed."

Jordan now tore along the banks of the river for miles and miles, about as far as from Nassereit to Siegmundsberg, where he found a weak bending board upon which he stepped, and plump down went the monster into the wild foaming water, in which he had to struggle for a long time ere he succeeded in reaching the opposite bank. Meanwhile the boys had got far in advance; but the giant ran as fast as he could, and soon caught sight of them again on the other side of a large lake which he did not know how to get over, as he had no idea of swimming, and wade through he dared not, as he did not know how deep it might be, and there was no boat either large enough to carry him over. Therefore he shouted again to the boys in a flattering tone, "Dear boys, tell me how you got over the lake!"

"The boys answered, "We have tied large stones round our necks, upon which we have swum across."

So he took a heavy rock and tied it firmly round his neck, jumped into the water, and was immediately drowned. So the boys escaped, and people say Fangga did not die of grief over the loss of her savage husband.

A few days afterwards Lorenz Mayrhofer, a friend of the farmer of Seehaus, returning from the market of Imst where he had sold a team of oxen, and carrying the yokes on his shoulders, stopped at Krapf's house on his way home, and over a glass of Tyrolian wine with which Hitte Hatte had herself served him, he said to his friend, "One sees most wonderful things in these times. After leaving the Döllinger Hof on my way here, a voice called out to me from the heights of the mountain, 'Carrier of the yokes, tell Hitte Hatte that she can now go home, for Jordan is dead.'"

The farmer and his wife looked at one another and then at Hitte Hatte, who, hearing the news, set down the ladle which she was holding, and said, "If Jordan is dead, then I am happy again. Take great care of the hairy house-worm. I thank you much for your kindness to me, and wish you all luck with your farm. If you had asked me more I should have told you more," and in saying so she passed out of the door, and has never again been seen.

The farmer, his wife, and friend were struck dumb with astonishment, and could not divine the girl's meaning. Under the " hairy house-worm," she had meant the cat. " What a pity it is," still now say the peasants of Strad, " that the (Seehaus farmer never asked more of the fairy, for if he had done so we should know more."

THE FISHERMAN OF THE GRAUN-SEE.

In following the valley of Etsch, and after leaving the village of Haid, the traveller arrives first at the lake called Haider-See, and then in about an hour's walking on the borders of the Graun-See, above which on the side of the mountain, lies, in a most picturesque situation, the little hamlet of Graun.

There every garrulous old woman or little village child can tell him how often when evening sets in the fairies have been seen floating like flickering candles round the lofty peak above, or heard singing sweetly on calm moonlight nights before the entrance to their caves. This spot on the mountain bears to the present day the name of Zur Salig (to the holy ones).

On a beautiful autumn evening some forty years ago, a fisherman in his little barque was setting his nets in the See. The night was mild and beautiful, and the air so clear and pure that he could distinctly hear the sheep-bells on the surrounding mountains, and the Angelus as it rang from the hamlets of Reschen, Graun, Haid, even as far as the distant village of Burgeis; and the sound of the bells of the monastery of Sancta Maria, which lies above it, came wafting solemnly and softly over the water. The moon rose slowly in silent majesty above the surrounding mountains, lighting up every distant peak, and turning the lake into a bed of liquid silver, and as the distant song of the Holy Fräulein struck the ear of the poor fisherman, he abandoned his nets and listened entranced.

The moonlight faded slowly away, and the dark-ness of night set in, yet still he remained motionless in his boat, dreaming of the angel's song he had heard from Heaven. Morning broke, and still he sat there with his hand on the rudder, and his eyes riveted on the abode of the Holy Ones. His com-rades came and called him, but he did not answer; they went to him and found him dead. He lies buried in the little churchyard of Graun, and every villager can point out his grave.

THE GIANTS HEIMO AND THÜRSE.

Out of the Neustädter-Thor of Innsbruck leads the Brenner-Strasse, close by the beautiful and rich Abbey of the Premontaries Wilten, called also Wiltau. On each side of the principal façade of the magnificent church of this ancient cloister are still to be seen the enormous stone statues of two giants who bear the names of Heimo and Thürse. Both giants belong to that age in which their huge race

first began to conform their rough nature to the
ideas of civilization, when Christianity entered into
the then impenetrable valleys of the Tyrol.

One of these enormous mountain giants of the
country was called Heime or Heimo, who was so tall
that he was obliged to raise the roof of his house so
that he could stand upright in it, and of the most
cruel and savage nature. The inhabitants of the
surrounding country dreaded him beyond measure,
and begged him to spare their farms and homesteads, offering to cede to him as much of their ground
as he liked to decide upon, and then, should he ask
it all, they would retreat and cultivate other parts
of the country. In answer to this proposition,
Heimo yelled, while pointing out an enormous rock,
" As far as I run with that stone upon my shoulders
so far is the ground my own." And saying so, he
seized the rock, walked up the little river Sill, turned
on the left to the Patscherkofl, went down through
Igels and round Wilten, and after having arrived
again at the point from which he had started, he
threw the stone with enormous force westward.
Then he began to build himself at the outlet of the
Sill valley, opposite the river Inn, an enormous

stronghold, for which he carried up huge rocks from the mountain clefts.

At that time there lived in the same valley another giant who was still taller and stronger than Heimo, and he had his abode high over Zirl, behind the jagged, bare, and steep peak of Solstein, upon the plateau of Seefeld, which he was the first to cultivate, and where now stands the hamlet of Tyrschenbach. Thürse, this was the name of this giant, hated Heimo, and took pleasure in always secretly destroying his newly commenced building; and when Heimo discovered who caused him all this damage, his gigantic fury awaked in him, and he went to attack Thürse, clad in light armour, and carrying an enormous sword. Thürse hearing the approach of Heimo, seized a ponderous beam, and then commenced such a terrible fight that the earth trembled, and rocks as huge as a tower detached themselves from the Solstein, and rolled down into the valley below. Blows fell as thick as hail, and at last the better armed Heimo was victor, for the savage Thürse succumbed to his enemy.

Just at that period (it was about the middle of the ninth century) a monk was preaching Christianity

in the valleys of the Sill, whom Heimo also went to
hear, and he felt sorry and repented having slain
Thürse.   He became a Christian, and was baptized
by the Bishop of Chur.   Then after having built the
existing bridge over the Inn, from which the city of
Innsbruck has taken its name, he renounced worldly
life, and instead of finishing his stronghold, he built
a monastery which is the still standing Wiltau or
Wildenau, commonly called Wilten.

This was a terrible disappointment to the devil,
who sent a huge dragon, of which there were already
at that time a great many in the Tyrol, to stop the
building of the monastery; but Heimo attacked the
dragon, killed him and cut out his tongue.   With
this huge tongue in his hand he is represented in
his statue; and the tongue, which is a yard and a
half long, has been preserved in the cloister up to
the present day.   Heimo became a monk at Wilten,
lived a pious life, and on his death was buried in
the grounds of the monastery.   The stone coffin in
which his gigantic bones repose is still to be seen
there, and it measures twenty-eight feet three inches.
Upon the coffin used to be his statue carved in
wood, which has since decayed, but there is still

hanging above it an ancient granite slab on which is recounted his history.

THE DRAGON OF ZIRL.

CLOSE to the bridge of Zirl, on the route to Inznig, in the Tyrol, lies the famous Dragon Meadow. The men of Inzing and Zirl remember still very well that when they were boys, an enormous thick long worm was washed by the swollen river Wildbach out of a cavern which stood on its banks, and which was called Hundstall. In this cavern the monster had resided for centuries, and had done endless damage in the surrounding country to both man and beast; he was generally called the dragon, and he killed and devoured all living creatures that ventured in his neighbourhood.

Through the cavern in the summer time flows a little stream which in the winter is almost quite dry, and so it was too at that time; but still it was strong enough to sweep the monster out, for when in the spring the warm weather suddenly arrived, the little stream became, from the melting snow, a

roaring torrent, which undermined the rocky cavern
of the dragon in the Hundstall, and swept out huge
pieces of rock together with the monster himself,
inundated the meadow, and left everything together
on the spot which has been called ever since the
Dragon Meadow. Even now the breach made in
the mountain by the torrent is to be seen.

The brute was a gigantic snake with the head of
a dragon, two large ears, and hideous fierce fiery
eyes. He was half dead when washed out of his
hole, but in spite of that he was seen writhing his
huge body about among the rocks. Nobody dare
approach him, so they shot him from a distance
with cannons. " He was a lindworm," said the old
mountaineer Mader of Zirl, who has hunted there
for more than sixty years, and who has faithfully
preserved this history. And as something to be
especially remembered, he added, " the half-dead
lindworm had gasped so fearfully that it had been
terrifying to see and listen to him, even from a distance." " One could not tell either," he said,
" whether he was not spitting venom," for even
now not an atom of green will grow on the meadow
where he died.

THE WANDERING STONE.

In the Zillerthal, about half an hour's walk from the little village of Fügen, in a small valley on the right-hand side of the entrance to the vast forest of Benkerwald, lies a piece of rock some two cubic feet in measure, bearing on its top side a rude cross chiselled in the stone. The rock is noted all over the country, for each time it is removed from its resting-place by some supernatural agency, it returns again to the same spot. Why it wanders in this strange manner nobody knows, but why it stands there is known to every little village child in the surrounding country.

At the end of the last century two peasant women of Fügen were engaged by the day in cutting corn at the adjacent farm of Wieseck, on the Pancraz mountain. The farmer, anxious to get in his corn while the fine weather lasted, promised to increase their wages if they hastened on with their work. At this promise both the girls redoubled their efforts, but at the end of the week instead of

C

paying them alike, the farmer in augmentation of
their wages gave to one of them two loaves of bread,
while to the other he gave but one. On their way
home close to Fügen, and on the spot where now
lies the stone, the two women began to quarrel
about the bread, and at last the dispute grew so
hot that they fell to fight with their sickles, and,
like tigresses, the sight of blood seemed only to increase their ferocity ; and what seems to be incre-
dible, but which is nevertheless perfectly true, they
fought until they both fell down and bled to death
on the spot. Here they were buried, and over them
was placed the stone which still remains there,
but none of the villagers will pass that way after
nightfall.

There are numberless people who have convinced
themselves of the wonderful property of the ' Wan-
delstein,' and many are the warnings given by the
country folk to travellers who seek to pass there
after the sun has set.

A TYROLIAN FORESTER'S LEGEND.

.

ONE day a poor woman of Lengenfeld, in the Oetz valley in the Tyrol, went up the mountains to meet her husband, who was guarding a flock of goats there. On her way she passed by a chapel into which she entered, and while she was praying a Lämmer vulture swooped down and carried off in his claws her little son, who was amusing himself outside on the moss. But Heaven ordained that the vulture should settle with his prey on a peak which was quite close to the goat-herd, who frightened him off with stones, and so, without knowing it, he became the preserver of his own child, whom he had not seen since the spring. Now it happened that three good fairies who resided in the neighbourhood of the Oetz-Thal, beneath an enormous mountain peak called the Morin, had been invisibly active in the saving of the goat-herd's boy.

The boy grew up and always bore in his mind an

c 2

attraction to the highest peaks of the mountains;
he became a hardy Alpine climber and clever
mountain shot, and as such a secret impulse ever
pushed him to the heights above Morin, for there—
so said the legend—was the Paradise of animals;
there were herds of gazelles and stone-bucks, and
no huntsman had ever succeeded in approaching
them. But the fool-hardy boy wished to try his
luck, and commenced his wanderings, which ended
by his getting lost, and being in danger of his life.
One day he didn't know where he was, and from
the ice-covered peak which reaches into the clouds
over ten thousand feet high, he slipped down upon
a green Alp which he had been unable to see from
above, and in that fall he lost his senses.

As he came again to himself he was lying on a
beautiful bed in the crystal cave of the three fairies,
who had saved him for the second time. They
stood round him shining with heavenly benevolence,
and love, and their look awakened in him the sweetest sensations. He remained now a well-cared-for
guest of the fairies, was allowed to look at their
beautiful abode, their gardens, and their pets; he
was told that his amiable hostesses were the pro-

tecting genii of all Alpine animals, and they made
him promise never to kill or to hurt one of those
innocent creatures,—no gazelle, no Alpine hare,
no snow-hen, not even a weasel. He was allowed
to remain with them three days, and had per-
mission to worship and adore them. But then
he was obliged to promise three things faithfully
and on his soul's salvation, if ever he wanted to
return to them, or, in case he never cared to do so,
if ever he wished to live happily down in the valley.
Firstly, he was bound to observe a silence as deep
as the grave that he had ever seen the three fairies
or been in their presence; secondly, they made him
swear the promise which he had already given, never
to do any harm to any Alpine animal; and thirdly,
never to let human eye see the way which they
were going to show him, and through which he
might be the more easily able to return to their
abode. A fourth promise they left to his honour,
without binding him down by oath or vow, and that
was to preserve the love which he had shown to
them, and never to have anything to do in any
way with any other girl. Then, after a tender part-
ing, the son of the Alps was taken into a steep

mountain gully which led down to the valley of the
rushing Achen, which tears along under bowers of
Alpine rose-bushes. After these injunctions, the
fairies told him that on every full-moon night he
was allowed to pay them a visit of three days'
duration, and that he had only to enter through
that gully, and give below a certain sign with which
they acquainted him.

The boy returned home completely altered; it
seemed as though he was dreaming, and soon
enough from every one he gained the name of the
'dreamer;' for henceforth he never took an Alpine
stock in his hand, never went hunting, and never to
a village dance, but every full-moon night he stole
quietly to the chasm in the rock, deep beneath the
Morin, entered into the interior of the mountain,
and was for three days happy with the fairies, to
whose wondrous songs he listened entranced. At
home his form shrank, he became pale and ema-
ciated, and it was in vain that his parents and
friends pressed him to tell what was the matter
with him. "Nothing at all," he always answered
to these questions; "I am as happy as I can be."

As his father and mother had become aware of

his secret strolls on the full-moon nights, they followed him once quietly, and close at the entrance
of the chasm his ear was struck by his mother's
voice, who called his name, and at the same moment
the rocks shut together before his eyes, and the
mountains crashed down with the noise of thunder,
so that rocks fell down upon rocks. The poor boy's
happiness was gone for ever. Troubled and abstracted, he returned to his native village; he cared
neither for his mother's tears nor his father's re-
proaches, and remained apathetic and indifferent to
everything; and so he faded away until autumn
arrived, until the herds were driven down into the
winter stables of the village, and the beautiful
summer life of the mountain world died and was
covered with snow.

Then one day two friends of the goat-herd arrived, and talked of a hunting excursion which they
intended to make on the top of the Morin; and then
for the first time again the eyes of the pale young
Alpine hunter became bright, the irresistible love
of hunting awakened again in him,—perhaps, too,
there was some greater attraction. He longed to
penetrate once more into the dominion of the fairies

be it even at the risk of his life. As to life, he no longer valued it, and death was a liberation.

The infatuated youth prepared his hunting things, borrowed an Alpine stock, for his own had been left behind broken in his fall from the peak of the Morin, and then he joined the hunting excursion which started in early morning. First he walked with them, then he hurried before higher and higher, as though he was attracted by the most irresistible power. His heart grew light as he ascended, for too long the heavy air of the narrow valley had oppressed him. He climbed as quickly as though he had eaten arsenic, that fearful poison which many an Alpine climber takes in the smallest quantities to make himself lighter, and at last he caught sight of a sentry gazelle, which whistled and disappeared behind the peak upon which it had been standing. The young Alpine hunter climbed to the top of the peak, from whence he saw down below him a little green spot, upon which were browsing, though far beyond his reach, a large herd of gazelles. Only one of them came within range, and this one he pursued pitilessly, until the poor animal in her anxiety and terror was unable to proceed further, and stopped on the edge of a precipice, which the huntsman in his excitement had never noticed. He levelled his rifle—the plaintive cry of a female voice resounded in his ears, but he paid no heed to it,—he took deadly aim and fired. Lo! at that moment he was surrounded by a halo of brightness, and in the midst of that brilliant light stood the gazelle unhurt, and before her floated the three fairies in dazzling splendour, but with severe and angry countenances. They approached him, but on seeing their faces without one smile or look of love upon them, the boy was seized with a deep horror. He staggered,—one step more, and backwards he fell down the precipice a thousand feet deep; and from the edge, where in falling his feet had stood, pieces of stone rolled down, and a tremendous wall of rock tore down after him with a fearful roar, and buried him for ever beneath its *débris*.

There still stands the rock, which is pointed out, even to this day as 'The Huntsman's Grave.'

THE PERJURER.

On the Kummersee, which is also called Hindersee, in the Tyrol, the parish of Schönna possesses two beautiful mountains which they had only hired in former times from the villagers of Passeir. But at last the inhabitants of Schönna affirmed that they were their own property, and therefore commenced a law-suit which was to be decided by oath. A man of Schönna committed perjury, which he thought to do safely in the following manner. He stuck in his hat a ladle called in the Tyrol schöpfer, which is also the German word for Creator, and put in his shoes some earth out of his own field. So he appeared on the Alp before the judges and swore: "As truly as I have the Schöpfer above me and my own earth beneath me, the two Alps belong to Schönna." In consequence of that oath they were awarded to the villagers of Schönna by the judges.

But at the same moment the devil flew down the precipices, seized the perjurer by his neck, and dragged him straight off to hell, leaving behind him as he rushed through the air a dreadful smell of sulphur and a train of fire. With his prey he beat an enormous hole through the Weisse Wand, a huge mountain close to the Kummersee, which hole is still to be seen up to the present day as a warning. From thence he flew over the Christl Alp down to the village of St. Martin, where he rested himself upon a stone, and then dragged the body through the mud of the village streets, and as he passed, the devil is said to have grunted, " For there is nothing so weighty as a perjurer's body."

THE BURNING HAND.

In the village of Thaur, near Salzburg, there lived about two centuries ago a good priest, who occupied his time in doing charitable works to all around. In the ruins of the once huge and superb castle of Thaur a hermit had founded his humble little cell, and both priest and hermit were the most intimate of friends, and had vowed to each other that he who should die the first, should appear to the other after death.

The poor hermit was very clever in making artificial flowers for the altar, and one night when busy with his work a knock came to his little window, and he saw the spirit of his friend who had died a few days before. At first he was greatly terrified, but pricking up his courage, he addressed the poor soul of the priest, who replied to him and said,

"You see I am dead in the body, but I have still to do penance, although I have faithfully fulfilled the commands of God and the Holy Church, have given alms according to my means, have instituted a perpetual mass in the church of Thaur, and another in the chapel of St. Romedius, and founded an everlasting fund for the poor. For three sins have I this penance to perform, one of omission and two of vanity; out of absence of mind I forgot to say a mass for which I had been paid, and I have been too vain of my fine white hands and beautiful flowing beard, and for this reason am I now compelled to suffer these torments. I pray you therefore to say in my stead the neglected mass," and the unhappy spirit of the priest recounted to the hermit the names of all those people for whom the mass was to be said, "Then, if out of charity to me you will fast, pray, and flagellate yourself, and help me in that way to do my penance, the time of my redemption will arrive much sooner, as if I had completed them all myself. It will also be a work of conciliation for me, if you will tell all I have just told you to my parishioners, so that they and my successors may take a warning from me, and think of me in their prayers."

The hermit answered, "I will most willingly fulfil all you ask of me and take upon myself every penance you desire; but if I tell all these things to your parishioners they will never believe me, and will jeer at me and say like the brothers of Joseph, 'Here comes the dreamer.'"

"Well, then, I will give you a sign of proof which will back up your words," answered the poor spirit e priest; "Give me something out."

The hermit then handed out the cover of a flower-box, upon which the shadow laid his hand, and returned it instantly to him; and lo! to his astonishment he found, deeply branded upon it, the imprint of the hand of the priest as though it had been done by a red-hot iron.

After this the hermit zealously commenced the charitable work of redeeming the soul of his faithful friend, and continued it many a month in saying masses, repeating prayers, and subjecting himself to the most severe flagellations, whilst from time to time the troubled spirit of the poor priest appeared to him in bodily form, but always lighter and more brilliant than before. The pious hermit almost succumbed under the dreadful effects of his severe penances, which he still carried on for more than a year, when the night of All Saints arrived, and again the poor soul of his friend appeared before him, now no longer poor, but in the splendour of transfiguration, and said, "I thank you, good friend. I am now redeemed; you too shall soon be released from your earthly bondage, and will return to God penanceless. I shall attend you there where there are no more sufferings," and in saying so he disappeared in the midst of a halo of glory.

Seven days afterwards the hermit died; and now in the charming little pilgrims' chapel of the holy Romedius, near Thaur, is to be seen, framed beneath a glass case, the wooden board bearing the brand of the burning hand, and with the duly attested inscription dated from 1679; also the bust of the priest with the beautiful hands and flowing beard.

The imprint of the Burning Hand took place on the 27th October, 1659, at midnight.

THE THREE FAIRIES OF THE UNGARKOPF.

BETWEEN the village of Imst and the railway station of Nassereit lies the Gurgl Thal (Gurgl valley), through which runs the little stream of the Pilger-bach. On the way from Imst to Nassereit stands the little hamlet of Strad, and on making the ascent from this hamlet up the Ungar mountain, or Ungarkopf, one arrives after an hour's walk at a vaulted grotto, which is the entrance to a vast cellular cavern noted in former times as the abode of three fairies, called by the villagers 'die Heiligen' (the Holy Ones). These fairies appeared from time to time at the entrance to their grotto, bleaching

linen and hanging out snow-white clothes in the
sun; they are said to have even come down as low
as Strad, and helped the village girls to spin, but
people were generally afraid of them, and they who
saw the clothes hanging out in the wind ran off in
terror.   In this grotto, which is generally called the
Eggerskeller, there is a small hole just large enough
for a child to creep through.

One day the cowherd of Strad went up the mountain to cut birch for brooms, and as the lovely
green before the grotto was just convenient for his
work, he sat down there, and stripping the leaves
from the branches, set about making his brooms.
On the following day when he returned to the same
spot on the same business, he found to his great
astonishment that every little leaf had been swept
away, and not a vestige of one of them left.   He
sat down on a rock and began his work, when all at
once he heard from the interior of the mountain the
voices of three girls, which sounded so charmingly
to his ears that he was quite entranced.   He listened and held his breath until the song finished,
and then he descended the mountain to the village
in a state of enchantment.

The cow-herd was soon afterwards on his favourite place, while his herd, guarded by his faithful dogs, browsed around him; and again he found the leaves he had left on the preceding day swept away; and as he looked up he saw three white robes floating in the wind, but as he could not see the cord upon which they ought to have been suspended, he was seized with an unutterable terror, and hurried away from the spot. "Had he only taken one of these dresses," still now say the superstitious people of Strad, "one of the Heiligen would have been bound to his service for ever."

Although the dresses had frightened the youth so much, an irresistible longing compelled him a few days afterwards to climb once more the Ungarkopf, where all at once one of the fairies appeared to him with love and joy beaming on her countenance, but she did not approach him, and it seemed rather as though she wished him to follow her, for she looked smilingly behind, entered into the mountain and disappeared from his gaze. He dared not follow her. Henceforth he listened only to their enchanting songs, which resounded from the interior of the mountain, and consumed himself in silent longing.

D

About fifteen years ago there lived in the village of Strad a peasant of the name of Anton Tangl, who is now dead. One day this peasant went up the mountain in the neighbourhood of the grotto, to dig up young fir-trees, which he intended to place round his Alpine hut. While digging up these trees, one of them was more firmly fixed in the ground than the others, and he was obliged to go very deep to get the tree up. When he lifted it out of the ground he discovered a deep hole, and looking down he saw far below a green meadow, through which trickled a milk-white rippling stream. At this the man was greatly astonished, but still more so when upon the green meadow far beneath him he saw on the grass, like little tiny dolls, the three fairies. They were sitting close to one another, interlaced together by their arms, and singing a sweet song whose air he could distinctly hear, without being able to catch the words. Tangl listened until nightfall, when he could no longer see into the interior of the mountain. Then he descended to the village, and recounted what an extraordinary thing had befallen him. But of course no one would believe, and therefore on the following day several of his friends went with him up the Ungarkopf. Tangl went on bravely before the others, and searched for the spot, but in vain; and he was now compelled to suffer the ridicule of his companions, who called him a fool, a liar, and a dreamer.

"If I had only held my tongue," Tangl used to say when he recounted this story, "and had entered into the mountains instead of telling others what I had seen, I should have been able to bring many precious things out of them, and should have been rich and happy all my life; but man after all is but a stupid animal."

THE GREEN HUNTSMAN.

In the village of St. Johann, in the lower part of the valley of the Inn in the Tyrol, the following incident took place some fifty years ago.

A girl who had been jilted by her lover refused to go to a wedding to which she had been invited by her neighbours, and where there was to be music and dancing. In her grief and despair she raged and noised about at home, until the evil one in the form of a green huntsman appeared before her, and invited her to the dance. Without reflecting any longer she went with him to the wedding-feast, glad that her unfaithful suitor should no longer enjoy his triumph. The huntsman danced so fast and so well that all the guests admired him, for he sang and was the most spirited among them all. But in spite of this, every one shuddered when they looked at him, for his mien was like that of a snake, sly and venomous. The girl, however, did not care at all about it, and enjoyed herself all the evening.

On their way home the huntsman asked the girl if she would allow him to serenade her on the following evening, to which she gave a most joyful assent. On the following night, just as the church clock was striking twelve, some one knocked at the girl's bedroom window. She opened the lattice to greet the huntsman, who now appeared before her in the devil's most hideous form. He seized upon her and dragged her fiercely through the narrow iron bars which guarded it, so that pieces of skin and flesh remained hanging on them, and the warm blood ran in streams down the wall. He then flew off with the screaming girl through the air.

Up to the present day it has been impossible to wash or rub those blood stains away, and any one who passes through the little village of St. Johann, can see them for himself.

THE TYROLIAN GIANTS OF ALBACH.

IN a wild mountain valley in which only savage animals and reptiles were to be found, and in which vast expanses of moss covered the swamps so treacherously that even bears and wolves had been engulfed in them, a huge giant arrived one day, looked at the surrounding country, and chose it for his abode. He dug himself a cave, built drains through which he sent off the superfluous water into the lower valleys; and as, after having chopped down enormous expanses of forest, he found that it had become quite to his taste, he set off in search of

a wife. He neither wished for a fairy nor a moonlight maid, and for that reason he went upon the
peaks of the mountains, from which he soon returned
with a giantess who was as strong and savage as
himself, and who assisted him dauntlessly in all his
abominable works.

In three years they were obliged to considerably
enlarge their habitation, as their three young
giant sons began to grow up; and when these
became strong enough, they helped their father to
build a new house. The old giant felled the trees
on the Alp Mareit, which stands about six miles
from his former abode, and his sons dragged the
trunks to the building-spot. They were not then
very strong, and could only drag one tree each at a
time, which, however, was no less than eight feet in
diameter. Only the youngest of the giant's sons,
whose name was Bartl, sometimes dragged two at
once, at which his father smiled with contentment.

To make his new residence like that of a civilized
family, the giant caught a few " flies," as he called
them, which were men and clever carpenters, who
were compelled to hew and shape the wood, in which
work the giant's sons helped in turning the trees,

as it would have been impossible for the carpenters to do it themselves.

People call the swamp which the giant has drained the Rossmoos, and to the giants they gave the name of the Rossmooser Riesen (Rossmoos giants), while the new house received that of the Rossmooser Hof (Rossmoos farm), which still stands upon the peak of Albach opposite Stolzenberg.

After the building had been finished a few years, the old giant father felt the approach of age in the gradual loss of his strength; therefore he began to think of making over his property to one of his sons. But he did not know to which of them to give it, as all three were equally dear to him, and at that time the laws of birthright were not yet introduced into the giant-race, no more than the institution which exists in other places, and according to which the youngest son receives the house, and pays to his other brothers their share in ready money. Therefore in his perplexity he talked it over with his wife, who advised him thus, " Give it to the strongest of them, and then you have done."

This idea pleased the giant very much, and that day at dinner he said to his sons, " Boys, I am old, and one of you shall have the house; but each of you is as dear to me as the other, and so I think you must decide it by throwing a stone, and the one who proves himself the strongest shall have the house."

This proposition was very acceptable to the giant's sons; and after the dinner was finished, the old fellow took a stone of 650 pounds into which was fastened an iron ring weighing 50 pounds, and carried it fifteen paces from the Hof, which fifteen paces made just one mile, as the giant with one step covered as much ground as would take a human being five minutes to walk. Now they proceeded to the trial according to the ancient rules of throwing stones, as it was invented centuries ago by the giants themselves. He who had to throw stood with the left leg firmly planted on the ground, while with the right foot, which was passed through the iron ring of the stone, he swung it against the mark, which in this case was the giant's Hof, and the stone was to alight on the other side of the house.

The eldest son commenced; he took up the stone and flung it, but it didn't even reach the mark, and fell far short into a fence, which it smashed to pieces. The second son then fetched the stone and tried his chance with more success, for he touched the house and knocked in the front wall.

"You stupid asses!" shouted the old man, "is that the best you can do?"

Now came the turn of the youngest, who did even better; for he threw the stone so vigorously and high that it fell on the top of the roof, through which it crashed like a bomb-shell and destroyed everything in the house.

"Oh, my Bartl!" sneered the angry old giant, "you are a clever fellow. You have gained the house, but now you will be obliged to repair it." And then he began to rave, "You sacrischen Sauschwänz, that you are. Now look at me, poor weak old thing, how I will beat you. Run, dear wife, and bring me back the stone."

His wife ran and brought him the stone on the little finger of her left hand, which just passed through the ring, and the old giant set himself in attitude according to the rules of the game. He hurled the stone with such tremendous force that it fell far on the other side of the Rossmooser Hof;

and seeing this the three young giants slunk off quite ashamed of themselves. The old giant sighed as he said, " There is really no strength left among the young folk. At one time one had no cause to be ashamed of himself. I remember still how I carried a stone weighing a hundred centner (10,000 pounds) from the Kolbenthalmelch place to the Kolbenthal saw-mill, where it is still lying ; you can go and look at it there, you Fratz'n."

At the same time as these giants were living at the Rossmooser Hof, there resided a couple of other giants upon the Dornerberg in the Zillerthal, who always cast angry looks at young Bartl, and challenged him very often to fight. Bartl avoided them as much as he could, and showed no inclination to measure his strength with them, for he had not a quarrelsome nature. One day the giants of Dornerberg met the Rossmooser Riesen with Bartl, at whom they sneered, and mockingly challenged him again to fight with them, but as Bartl was undecided and would not answer, the old giant became angry with his son and said, " You are then no bub (boy) at all, that you suffer all this."

" Should I fight them ? " asked Bartl, and as his

father nodded his head he added, " But, father, it's not worth my while to fight one alone, so I shall fight them both at once."

The fight then began, and Bartl instantly seized upon the two Dornerberg giants by the collar, held them up, beating the air with their hands and feet, until their eyes streamed with water; he then dashed them on the ground where they lay stunned, and it was only with the greatest trouble that they were restored to life. When they came to their senses, they stole away from the scene of the fight quite ashamed of themselves, and made up their minds never again to have anything to do with Bartl, whose fame, after this tremendous victory, spread far and near through the country; for the Dornerberg giants were in no way weak, since each of them carried seven to eight centners (600 to 700 pounds) from Zell, in the Zillerthal, up the Dorner-berg, where they lived in a deep cavern. With this huge weight they sprang lightly from stone to stone in the river which runs through the valley, and even stooped down and caught the trout in their hands as they passed over.

THE WITCH'S VENGEANCE.

AT Sterz, about an hour's walk from Brixen, on the line from Innsbruck to Verona, close beneath the mountain called Rodeneck, there lived some fifty years ago in a fine farm-house a well-to-do young couple with one child. In all the villages round about an old beggar woman was much dreaded as a witch, and this woman came very often to the farm begging. The good people of the farm used to give her directly all she desired, just to rid themselves of her importunities. But one day the farm-labourers made up their minds to discover whether the old hag was really a witch or not, and after she had entered the room, they set a broom on end before the door. It was on a Saturday evening. When a broom is put upside down before a door—such is the superstition of the people—the witch cannot get out again.

When the hag therefore tried to get out, she saw the trick, and remained in the room until late at night. At last she said angrily to the peasant's wife, " Sweep out the room ; it is Saturday evening, and how comes it that you leave the room so long unswept ? "

This she repeated many times, but always to no purpose, for the peasant's wife knew about the trick ; but when she saw that the hag was becoming tremendously angry and fierce, she was dreadfully frightened, and ordered the servant to take the broom and sweep out the room. Directly the servant took up the broom and removed it from the door, the hag darted out full of venom, hatred, and spite, and the most revengeful determinations.

And what a vengeance this was ! She dried the cows, brought down storms and destroyed the crops, made their child hopelessly ill so that it died ; the poor farmer went into a decline through grief, and his wife was misled over the Rodeneck by the diabolical creature, and broke both her arms and legs.

So cruel is the vengeance of a witch.

THE PIOUS HERDSMAN.

ABOUT three miles above Uderns, in the valley of the Ziller, lies the Asten or Voralp, also called the Stuben, upon which a poor spirit used to wander, seeking its redemption.

The proprietor of the Asten was unable to find any one who would undertake to guard his cattle on the mountain, for every one was afraid of the ghost. At last, a poor brave boy offered himself for this purpose, and was of course gladly accepted.

One day as he was driving his cows upon the mountain, he saw a tall dark figure wandering about a few steps from the door of his little hut, which is called in the Tyrolian dialect the schlamm. The boy instantly spoke to the apparition, and asked whether he could not do anything to release him from his pain, to which the ghost answered, yes, he could, if during a whole year, without omitting one single day, he would devoutly repeat a rosary, and promise during that time never to swear or do a bad action, and always to say the rosary at the same hour every day.

The honest son of the Alps conscientiously fulfilled his duty for a very long time, until one day in the summer a pretty little village girl came up the mountain and begged the cowherd to stand godfather to her sister's child, for they were very poor, and knew no one who would be likely to accept the office but him. The good herd promised directly that he would; and when the day of the baptism arrived, he well fed his cows and then set off down the mountain to Uderns. After the ceremony was over, he had intended to return immediately up the Asten, as it is the custom in the Tyrol to feed the cattle four times a day. But the mother of the child implored him to remain a little longer with them, and so one thing and another prevented him from starting so soon as he had wished. It happened therefore that he remained in the village until evening had set in, for they insisted on serving him with good liqueurs, which to the poor cowherd were a great treat, as it is very seldom one of his position has the chance of tasting such a thing. At last he set off on his return, and as he climbed the mountain he remembered that he had forgotten the hour of his prayers, and was so grieved at this omission, that he cried bitterly, and repeated aloud the neglected rosary as he went along. Then the idea struck him that he would also offer up his baptismal work for the benefit of the poor spirit.

When he arrived at his hut he proceeded immediately to the stables, thinking to himself, "how hungry the poor cattle must be," but great was his astonishment when he saw that the best food had been placed before them, and that everything was in the most perfect order; but far greater was his surprise when after he had retired to rest, the poor spirit appeared before him, clad in snow-white garments, and told him that he was now redeemed, and that which had been principally instrumental in his redemption, was the offering which the good cowherd had made of the baptism of the child. After this the spirit disappeared, and has never been seen again. Since this fact became known, it has been, and still is the custom in all parts of the Tyrol for godfathers and godmothers to make an offering of the baptismal rite on behalf of the poor souls in purgatory.

THE ADASBUB.

ABOUT sixty years ago there lived at Lengenfeld, in
the valley of the Oetz, a man of enormous height,
called generally " the Adasbub," who was a perfect
monster, besides being a thief, glutton, sot, and
fighter. He had been among the soldiery, and
fought in many wars, from which he had returned
still more savage and wild than ever; he had
brought home large sums of money from foreign
countries, which he had stolen and extorted from
people, and now he bought a farm of his own,
which he began to manage, though more like a
pagan than a Christian. He never went to church,
but was always to be seen in the village inn, where
he boasted the first in Lengenfeld about his velvet
jacket decorated with buttons made out of old
pieces of silver money. The young fellows of the
village soon became ashamed of their clothes, and
wished to imitate the vain ideas of their paragon.*

* In the Tyrol it is the custom for the peasants to have
their jackets and waistcoats decorated with rows of silver

E

The Adasbub was besides of enormous bodily strength, and had already at once defeated fifty men, who had attacked him; and he who offended him had to fear lest this dreaded man might go, as if by accident, and turn a mountain torrent upon his farm, or roll down huge snowballs, with most likely rocks hidden in them, upon his roof.

His whole pleasure and only occupation was to swear, drink, bluster, and injure his neighbours; he surrounded himself with a gang of fellows who suited his tastes, and was their leader in carrying out the most fearful outrages. They tore the doors of the peaceful inhabitants from their hinges, and carried them away into the forests; hoisted the farmers' carts upon the roofs of their houses; stole the wine from the sacristies, which they drank to the perdition of the priests; shut up goats in the little field chapels, and pulled down the crosses in the cemetery, which they stuck upside down in the ground over the graves, and boasted in their

buttons, which are sewn on in such a manner that they over-lap each other. These buttons, of which they are very proud, are all made of old silver money, and each row contains from fifteen to twenty of them.

wickedness that they were making Christendom
stand upon its head.

A newly-concocted villany was to be carried out
in a farm, which stands upon the Burgstein, above
Lengenfeld, and it had reference to the farmer's
daughter; but the farmer came to hear of it, and
determined to defend his home against the outrages
of these cowardly villains. So he sharpened his
axe, and as the Adasbub entered the house, he
brought it down with tremendous fury upon the
head of the monster of iniquity, who fell dead at his
feet with a split skull. On seeing their leader re-
ceive this unlooked-for welcome, his companions
took refuge in flight, and there was an instant
alarm throughout the country. People from all
parts swarmed up the Burgstein, and thanked the
farmer for having delivered the country from such a
wretch.

They cut off the head of the Adasbub, and
dragged the body to the edge of a precipice, from
which they pitched it down on to the road, which
passes by a now much frequented sulphur bath,
called the Rumunschlung. The head was thrown
into the charnel-house of the cemetery of Lengen-

feld, where it still lies, a terror and warning to all wicked men. The skull is nearly cloven in two, and from time to time, at certain midnights, it gets red hot all over, and is then horrible to look at. Many people say that when it is burning, it rolls from the charnel-house into the chapel, in which it turns round and round in a circle, and then jumps again back to its place, where it slowly cools, and next day it looks again just like any other skull.

THE WHITE SNAKE.

CLOSE to Mitterwald, on the little river Eisach, rises on the right-hand side of the village the enormous mountain called the Mitterwalder Alp, upon which, on account of the great number of venomous snakes which were there, no cattle could be pastured. The majority of these were huge white reptiles, of which the people were particularly fearful. About fifty years ago there arrived in the country one of those students, or as they called them, " Fahrende Schüler " (wandering collegians), to whom people used to attribute supernatural power, and the peasants asked him to rid them of the plague of snakes.

The student promptly assented to their request, and went up the mountain, where he made a circle upon the Alp-meadow, and ordered the peasants to plant a tree in the middle of the ring; then he climbed the tree, and by his incantations he charmed all the snakes into the large fire which he had lighted around it. But all at once a huge snake hissed loudly and fiercely, and on hearing this the student cried out, " I am lost ; " and at the same moment a white snake darted with the swiftness of an arrow through his body, and he fell dead from the tree, and was consumed in the fire.

Those who recounted this tale added, " It was a hazel-worm, for only those snakes have the power to dart through the air like an arrow and pierce through people's bodies." On the spot where this accident took place, and where the student made the fiery circle, there has never since an atom of grass grown again.

It is asserted the blindworms had once the same power, until it was taken away from them by the

Blessed Virgin, who has caused them ever after-wards to remain sightless.

THE SCHACHTGEIST.

ABOUT an hour's walk from Reit, on the left-hand side of the entrance to the valley of the Alpbach, is situated a farm which bears the name of Larcha, and close to this farm is a deep mine in the side of the mountain, which at the time of this legend was being worked, and it was called the Silber Stollen (silver mine) of the Illn. Nine miners were employed in working the mine, and in it resided a Schachtgeist (mine ghost), who showed to the poor honest miners the richest lodes of silver. Their luck was extraordinary, and huge bars of the precious ore were carried every day out of the mine; and as the men worked on their own account, they soon became enormously rich, and for this reason they became also very dissolute and profligate. They were no longer content with their simple miners' attire, but bought fine clothes; they would no longer wear their grey blouses, but they would have velvet and rich cloth, and their wives went about dressed up in the most gorgeous colours.

The proverbially simple Alpböcker Tracht (costume of the Alpböck) was entirely set on one side by them, and a new fashion introduced; besides that, all sorts of iniquities were practised by them, which it would be impossible to describe.

This made the benevolent Schachtgeist intensely angry; he became fierce and savage, and when he appeared at the entrance of the mine his mien foreboded anything but good. Meanwhile the miners went on more badly than ever, and got so extravagant in their notions, that they even cleaned their tables and chairs with bread-crumbs. One day the farmer of Larcha was standing taking the fresh air at his door; the clouds foreboded a thunderstorm, and the air was dark and heavy. He had been working with his men down in the cellar, from which they could distinctly hear the noise of the miners' hammers, as they shouted and sung over their work. All at once the Schachtgeist passed by the door of the farm, and called out to the farmer in a terrible voice, " Shut your doors, and misfor-

tune shall escape you; I am away to the Illn to
silence the miners." The terror-stricken farmer
crossed himself, and on his knees implored Divine
protection, while the ghost tore up the mountain,
and then he shut his doors and returned to his
work. Not long after, the farmer and his men
heard fearful shrieks, which were immediately followed by a crash like thunder, which shook the
earth, and made the cellar in which they were
working tremble. They rushed up into the farmer's
room, and began to repeat the rosary, and as the
noise abated they went to bed.

On the following morning the news of a terrible
calamity spread far over mountain and valley.
The miners had been buried in the mine by an
earthquake, and their shrieking wives rushed wildly
about, rolling in the dust, and, in their agony and
despair, they nearly tore off the feet of the crucifix
which stands just above the farm on a cross-road.
But still more horrible was it when it was discovered that the buried miners were alive in their
prison, and screaming for help in the depths of the
mountain. For ten long days the terrible scene
lasted; when at last, after having worked night and

day, the villagers succeeded in entering the passage in which the miners were entombed; but there
a horrible spectacle presented itself to their eyes.
Over the dead bodies of the nine miners was sitting the Schachtgeist, covered with blood, and
terrible to look at, with the visage of the devil, and
glowering at the victims of his just wrath and judgment. The miners had been starved to death, and
were holding the leather of their shoes in their
teeth, after having gnawed their fingers to the
bones.

Every one who wanders over the mountain, and
passes by the farm of Larcha, can hear this dreadfully true legend, up to the present day, from the
farmer, who is the son of the man who was witness
of the fact. And if after the evening Angelus has
rung, by any chance a door in the farm remains
open, the housewife directly calls out, " Shut the
door, so that misfortune may escape us."

THE THREE BROTHERS.

At Reut, a village between Unken and Lofer, lived
a peasant who had three sons. The two eldest of
these were hardy gazelle hunters, and feared God as
little as they did the dangers of the mountains;
but the youngest was better, and different from his
brothers; he took interest in the farm, though now
and then he was induced by them to accompany
them to the chase. So it happened once that he
went with them to the high mountains, and on a
Sunday they were already standing high on the
peaks when the day dawned, and at that moment
they heard the Angelus ringing from the village of
Unken. The younger huntsman implored his
brothers to return, so that they might be in time
for church; but as they would not go, he did not go
either.

As they mounted higher and higher they heard
the mass bells ringing at Unken; the youngest
brother said, " Let us go back." But the others
jeered at him and said, " The whistle of a gazelle is

more to our taste than the mass bells and sermon."
When the enthusiastic huntsmen had arrived on
the very top of the mountain, the bells rang again,
and the youngest brother said, " Listen, there is the
elevation, we ought to have been there."

But his brothers sneered at him, and replied, " A
fat gemsbock here is much more to our mind than
the body of the Lord in the village church below."
These words were scarcely out of their mouths,
when clouds as black as ink enveloped the mountains, and everything became dark as night; then
came on a thunderstorm, as though the world was
at its end. After the storm was over the three
brothers were found on the peak of the mountain,
turned into stones in the form of gigantic rocks,
and there they still stand, known to every little
Tyrolian child under the name of "the Three
Brothers."

THE FIERY BODY.

Round about the village of St. Martin, in the Passeierthal, the parish comprises a great many single-lying farmsteads, which are dispersed about to the north in every direction for seven or eight miles towards the parish of Platt. In one of these farms a man was lying very ill, because on a Sunday, instead of going to church, he had hunted in the neighbouring forest, and had slightly wounded his foot with the iron heel of his other boot. It seemed as though the wound was poisoned, for it grew continually worse and worse, and at last threw the man into a deadly fever. The neighbours implored him to give up his evil ways, for he was a wicked fellow, and took delight in mocking at religion, and always, above every other, chose a Sunday or *fête* day for his hunting excursions.

But, wishing to appear an *esprit fort*, he answered that he preferred to arrange his own affairs with the Creator without their interference. In spite of all this, a good priest tried to persuade him out of his evil ways; but the wicked man replied to his exhortations by throwing a plate at him, out of which he had just been eating his milk soup. He remained obstinate and hardened, "determined," as he called it, to the last.

One day, when he was dying, the people of the house ran down to the priest, and implored him to come and save the unhappy sinner if it was still possible. The good priest, accompanied by his sacristan, hastened directly up the mountain, carrying the Holy Sacrament with them. As they arrived close to the farm, they were met by a fiery red body rushing through the air, spitting flames as it flew. It aimed directly at the priest, and was the body of the unbelieving Sabbath-breaker, who had died without repentance. The sacristan fell to the earth terror-stricken; but the priest said, "Fear not, Christ is with us," and as he spoke these words the fiery body rushed by, leaving them unhurt, and hurled itself down the fearful precipice of the Matatz valley.

THE VENEDIGER-MANNDL UPON THE SONNWENDJOCH.

NOT many years ago a little man of Venice, Venediger-Manndl, as he was called, clad in dark clothes, arrived in the Tyrol to gather gold bars, gold sand, and gold dust, out of the streams of the mountains; he was always seen in the small valleys, and especially on the Sonnwendjoch; he arrived in the spring, and went away again in the autumn. He was a good-hearted quiet little fellow, and on his way home he always passed the night in the hut of the herd who lived upon the adjacent Kothalp, near the Sonnwendjoch, which belongs now to Praxmarer, the innkeeper of Reit. Now it happened that the honest old herd of the Kothalp died, and his hut was taken by a wicked old man. The Venediger-Manndl entered as usual into the hut to pass the night, but the new herd, pushed on by the devil of avarice, made up his mind to kill him in the night, and to appropriate all his wealth. But the little herd-boy warned the gold-finder in time to enable him to save himself. Since then he has never been seen again.

The little herd-boy grew up, and became later on a servant at Isarwinkl, in Bavaria, where he afterwards became a soldier, and marched with the army into Italy. His regiment was stationed at Venice, and a few days after his arrival in the city he walked, full of curiosity, slowly along the beautiful palaces which stand on the canal, when all at once he heard his own name called from a window on the first story of one of them, and a person beckoned him to come up. He ran quickly up the wide marble stairs, and was received on the top by a noble Venetian, richly dressed in black velvet, who conducted him into a splendid apartment, and told him to take a place upon a sofa; then sitting down at his side, he said, " Years ago you saved the life of a Venetian upon the Kothalp, and now you are going to be rewarded ; so let me know your wish, and all you want you shall have."

" Let that be, kind sir," answered the soldier ; " I did but my duty, Heaven will recompense me if I have deserved it."

This answer seemed to please the Venetian, who

took the young man by the hand while saying,
"That shows me that you are a real Tyrolian."
Then he entered into a little side-room, and soon
afterwards returned in the dress in which he had
appeared as Venediger-Manndl on the Kothalp.
The soldier instantly recognized him, and was re-
joiced at meeting him. Now the Venetian repeated
his offer of gold and riches, but the soldier once
more declined, and answered, "Health and contentment are my riches, and that God will grant me as
long as he sees it fit to do so; though I have one
wish, after all, which is to be free of my service in
the army, so that I could go back to Isarwinkl,
where I have my love, a girl like milk and blood."

The Venetian had scarcely heard this wish, when
he took directly a large white cloth, in which a
mantle was wrapped; he took out the mantle, put
it over the shoulders of the soldier, and then covered it with the white cloth. All at once the
soldier felt himself rising in the air. "Greet your
love from me" were the only words he could catch
from the Venetian; for like an arrow he was borne
away through the high and grated bow-windows
which are used at Venice, the white cloth envelop-

ing him like a soft cloud, carried him along swiftly and gently, and set him down before the house of his love. In the pocket of the mantle he found a rich bridal gift.

Happiness never deserted the young fellow; he became very soon a happy husband, and bought himself out of the army, and since then he has often recounted this adventure.

HAHNENKIKERLE.

IN the hotel of the 'Golden Star,' at Innsbruck, there once arrived a very rich foreign Princess, who was suffering from a terrible disorder, which had baffled the efforts of every doctor to cure. Dr. Theophrast, of whom the Princess had heard, and whom she had come to Innsbruck to consult, declared that it was a malady over which he had no control, although he was a "Wonder Doctor." This was a great loss to the Doctor, and a terrible shock to the Princess, who had travelled so far in hopes of a cure.

F

One day when she was lying inconsolable in her bed, a little tiny man came into the room, who offered his services and gave her a potion, which he told her would restore her to health. But the little fellow added that on that day year he should return, and if she had forgotten his name, which was "Hahnenkikerle," she must promise to marry him, and to live with him under the Höttinger Klamm. The Princess gladly accepted this proposition, and she awoke on the following morning as fresh and healthy as a May rose.

She remained in Innsbruck, where she gave feast after feast, and in this way the year soon passed by. All at once she remembered her promise to the little dwarf, whose name had escaped her, and every effort to recall it was in vain. She asked many people, but no one could tell her; she confided her anxiety to her friends, but, of course, they could neither help her nor give her any advice. Only a poor servant girl, who came to hear of it, determined to try and help the good Princess. So she went into the Klamm, hoping to hear something certain there; she listened, and crept about all over, and at last she heard in the depth of the Klamm a joyous shouting, and down below she saw the dwarf jumping and singing, "Hurrah! the Princess in the 'Star' doesn't know that my name is Hahnenkikerle." The girl hurried home as fast as she could, and told the Princess all she had heard. Now the Princess remembered the name, and when the day came and the dwarf appeared, she called out to him, "Hahnenkikerle;" at hearing this the dwarf rushed away raging into the mountain.

The girl was rewarded by the Princess; and when she married an honest burgher of Innsbruck, she received a princely dower.

THE SORCERER OF SISTRANS.

IN Sistrans, a village close to Innsbruck, there lived, some sixty years ago, a man who was noted in all the surrounding districts for his evil and quarrelsome disposition. He attended every Kermesse and village meeting at which it was the custom of the blackguards of the surrounding

country to go and fight, but he never found one
who could master him.

This superhuman strength was not his only dis-
tinguishing quality, for he was well up in other
more doubtful arts, and was able to do rather more
than "boil pears without wetting the stalk."
Should a fine fox or a fat hare be running in the
forest close by, he set his traps just behind his
stove, and in the morning the game was sure to be
caught. Should anything have been stolen, people
came to him, for he had means of compelling the
stolen goods to be restored. For this purpose, he
merely took a little book bound in pigskin out of
his box, and began to read; and wherever the thief
might be, he was forced by some irresistible power
to take the stolen goods upon his back and bring
them before the sorcerer, by whom the proprietor
must always be present. This little book had such
a power that, at each word read by the sorcerer
from it, the thief was obliged to make a step; and
three times woe to him who had stolen something
which was heavy, or was obliged to bring his bur-
den from a long distance, or over steep mountains,
while the man was reading; from far off his pant-

ings could be heard, and he was drenched in perspiration when he arrived at the spot.

One day the sorcerer made himself a footstool of nine different sorts of wood, upon which he knelt down close to the organ in the church, and looked down upon the people, and there saw all the old hags and witches as they stood at the lower end of the church. After the service was over, these old hags set upon him in herds, and would have torn him to pieces had not the priest come in time to his rescue, for the hags now discovered that he had found them out.

This man had once on Christmas Eve stolen the consecrated Host, while the priest held it up after the consecration, and carried it with him, wrapped in a little piece of cloth always hidden on his left arm. From this proceeded all his unsurpassable tricks and indomitable strength. But at last came the " Scythesman Death," who cast him down upon the bed of sickness, and, in spite of all his strength and cleverness, he was bound to die; but that was a very hard thing for him. Three long days and nights the quarreller lay in the last agony without being able to die. Several times the priest came to him, and at last, after long exhortations and prayers, the dying man made a confession.

The Host, which had already grown into the arm, was cut out, and all the books and writings belonging to the art of sorcery which could be found were burnt; and as they were thrown into the flames it roared and thundered dreadfully, and there was such a terrific heat that the lead in the window-frames melted and ran down in streams, and during this hellish noise the sorcerer died.

THE GIANT SERLES.

On the Brennerstrasse, which leads out of Innsbruck, three huge scarped mountains raise their lofty peaks above the road, and these peaks are also plainly visible from the Inn valley, through which the railway to Innsbruck now runs.

There once lived in the neighbouring valley of the Sin a " Wilder," or wild man of enormous stature, who was a dreaded King of the Mountains. He was of a most extraordinarily savage nature, his wife as bad as he was, and his secret counsellor still worse than both. The King was passionately fond of hunting; and when on the track of a flying stag, he cared so little about anything but his own pleasure that he would dash, accompanied by all his followers and hounds, through the flocks and herds pastured on the mountains, carrying death and ruin wheresoever he went. Should the poor hunted animal by chance seek refuge among a herd, the demoniacal monster would take delight in urging on his bloodthirsty hounds to tear everything to pieces; and did the unfortunate herdsmen only try to make any remonstrance, they instantly shared the fate of their unfortunate animals, and were dragged to pieces on the spot by the savage dogs. On these occasions the giant, whose name was Serles, used to shout with joy, "Lustig gejaid" (bravely on), and neither man nor beast were able to defend themselves for a single moment against his fury. His wife and counsellor always accompanied him upon these excursions, and urged him on by their taunts to further excesses.

One day when they were out on one of their favourite expeditions, and the dogs had not only torn to pieces a poor stag, which had taken refuge among a herd of cows, but had also furiously attacked the herd itself, the herdsmen tried to drive them off, and one of them unslinging his cross-bow, in his anger, shot a dog dead upon the spot. At this the infuriated giant, excited beyond measure by his wicked wife and villanous counsellor, set the whole pack of hounds upon the unhappy herdsmen, and laughed with savage delight as he saw them torn limb from limb by the dogs. But in the midst of this terrible crime, Heaven's wrath fell heavily upon them. A terrific thunderstorm burst over their heads, and when it had passed away no more was to be seen of King Scrles, his wife, or his counsellor, but, in their stead, three huge glaciers rose into the clouds on the spot on which their iniquity had taken place. The one in the middle is the wicked monster Scrles, and to his right and left stand his cruel wife and inhuman counsellor.

Teamsters who pass along the Brennerstrasse on stormy nights even now often hear the howling of unearthly dogs, and, during storms, thunderbolts are constantly seen striking the " Rock Giants."

LEGENDS OF THE ORCO.

THE Tyrolians believe in the existence of the Orco, who is accounted to be a huge and powerful mountain ghost, who never ages; he is said to reside generally in the clefts and chasms of the precipices between Enneberg Abbey and Buchenstein and the surrounding mountains. He adopts every form, and exercises his enormous strength only in destroying. Everything he does is for the terror and annoyance of mankind; he very seldom takes the human form, and when he does it is of gigantic stature, with the most malevolent, wild, and cruel expression; he is then dressed in the manner of the giants, or quite naked, but covered thickly with hair, like the coat of a bear.

The following legends, collected on the spot, give a few instances of when and where he has been seen :—

THE Innkeeper, Anton Trebo, in Enneberg, who died in the year 1853, was a firm-minded man and noted as a great quarreller; he was sharp and enterprising in his business, and laughed to scorn all his guests when they ventured to recount anything about the Orco, who was held in most terrible dread by all the inhabitants of the surrounding country. Anton Trebo used to say that he believed in no apparition from either heaven or hell.

It was in the year 1825 that he returned from the market of St. Lorenz in his cart, with his son Franz. As he arrived at the rock called "Delles Gracies" (Rock of Grace), where in the hollow niches of the rock still stand many carved wooden statues of Christ and His saints, and just as he passed by, there all at once appeared a huge monstrous black dog, which ran round his cart and horses, and looked so diabolically that even the otherwise courageous bully was almost terrified. He held the reins tightly, and said to his son, " What is the dog doing there ? Drive him away." Franz tried to frighten the brute off with stones and blows, but the dog would not move, and Trebo, becoming more and more frightened, made the sign of the cross, and all at once the dog disappeared before their eyes.

Since this adventure, the innkeeper of Enneberg, believed firmly that it had really been the Orco, and has always defended his conviction of the existence of this fearful mountain ghost. Franz has taken the place of his father, and is now innkeeper of Enneberg, where one of his brothers lives with him.

In 1816 a brave peasant woman of Brenta, in the valley of Buchenstein, whose name was Maria Vinazzer, went with her son, who was nine years old, to meet her herd of cows which were returning from the Crontrin Alp. It was a beautiful autumn day, and they advanced the more gaily, as they were accompanied by the worthy parish singer, Lazar. As they arrived on the mountain side, all at once a wild horse trotted before them so suddenly that it appeared as though he had sprung from the ground, and wherever he trod fire played round about his heels.

Lazar, who was a courageous mountaineer, threw stones at the brute, but they rebounded from his sides, as though he had thrown them at a rock.

The horse would not be driven away, and always galloped before them. On seeing this extraordinary apparition, Maria said, "This is certainly the Orco, and if he meets the herd he will surely disperse it, as he has often done, and the cows will run in all directions over the precipices and chasms." They all three crossed themselves and repeated a prayer.

At that moment they arrived at the cross-way, called Livine, where stands a crucifix, and as the Orco approached near to it, he disappeared as suddenly as he had appeared; he neither sank into the earth, nor flew away through the air, but like a soap-bubble he vanished in an instant.

All three stood and prayed a little time before the cross, where the herd soon after gaily arrived, and the pious mother said joyfully to her son, "Look, dear child, he who is with God is everywhere safe, and no Orco or other evil spirit can harm him."

FROM the village of St. Kassian a young fellow went one evening to a distant farm to visit his sweetheart, and it was getting already dark. The youth heard several times the Orco calling out from a distance, but he paid no attention to it, and continued quietly his way. All at once he saw a little empty cart, dragged by four cats, run across the road; at this sight he was rather frightened, but still continued his way, not being able to make out what it all meant, when, on a sudden, there arrived a big black dog, with fiery lynx eyes, which grew bigger and bigger the nearer he came. "That is the Orco," thought the boy; so he crossed himself, and ran home as fast as his legs could carry him.

The dog bounded constantly after him for about a distance of three miles, and his fiery tongue hung for more than half a yard out of his jaws. The saliva which dropped from his mouth was like blue flaming fire, and burned like sulphur, filling the air around with a suffocating smell. The boy reached home, unharmed by the dog; but he had run so hard that his lungs became diseased, and he was always suffering, till death released him a few months afterwards.

"The cats which dragged the cart over the road,"

said the people who recounted this legend, " were hags, of whom there were thousands about at that time."

ONE day two young men of Ornella, in the Buchenstein valley, started on a brilliant night to pay a visit in a neighbouring village to their loves. They had scarcely left home when they noticed that they were followed by the gigantic Orco, in the form of a wild bull, who first walked quietly behind them, and then, as they began to run, changed himself into a huge ball, which rolled after them, bounding over high rocks, and alighting again on the ground close to them, with so much force and such a terrible noise that they were afraid of being crushed to death.

In their anxiety, they took the way over the meadows to the village of Valazzo, and jumping over the fence, which they had no time to open or break down, fell into the yard, at the foot of a large crucifix, which stands there, and embraced the cross, in a dying condition, with their arms. The Orco appeared at the fence, though now in human form ; but the poor youths were so terrified that they dare no longer regard him, and therefore were unable to describe his appearance. He beat with his hands upon the fence-bars so furiously, that the marks of his blows remained for years afterwards, as though they had been branded in by red-hot irons, until the wood decayed and a new fencing had to be put up ; but the saving cross still stands upon the same spot.

A PEASANT boy of Enneberg, walking through the deep and vast forest of Plaiswald, heard from afar the voices of men shouting, and took them for wood-cutters, so, according to the usage of the country, he answered them, and shouted several times just in the same tones as the voices he had heard. But then the horrible idea rushed into his mind that it might have been the Orco, and, at the same instant, he heard it quite close, for if one imitates the Orco, the monster arrives as fast as lightning. The youth tried to run away, but he felt as though petrified ; all around him became darkness, and he fell sense-less to the ground.

On the following day, when he came to himself,
he discovered that he was in the forests of Wellschellen, on the highest peak of the mountain, and
it became clear to him that the Orco had carried
him there, although the forests of Wellschellen
were on the other side of terrifically deep chasms
and precipices, into which the Orco would most
certainly have thrown him, had the peasant boy been
a godless fellow. He returned home, covered with
bruises and scratches, for Orco had torn him in such
a terrible manner that to the end of his days he
never attempted again to imitate the voice of any
one in the forests. The way over which the Orco
dragged the peasant is a good seven miles.

BIENER'S WIFE.

In the ancient castle of Büchsenhausen, which
stands just above Innsbruck, still wanders about
the apparition of one of its former possessors.
The legend does not say to whom the castle originally belonged, but old chronicles relate that it

passed, in the sixteenth century, into the hands of the celebrated iron-founder, Gregor Löffler, who gave it the name of "Büchsenhausen" (home of guns), because he had established there a gun-foundry. Later on it fell into the power of the reigning family of Austria, and the Archduchess Claudia presented it to her favourite Chancellor, Wilhelm von Biener, a liberal-minded nobleman, gifted with the doubtful talent of writing the most cutting satires, whose venomous point he turned against the nobility and church, and, for this reason, he brought upon himself the hatred of all those against whose opinion he wrote; but the favour of the Archduchess protected the talented statesman, who was most faithfully devoted to her interests.

On the 2nd of August, 1648, the Archduchess died, and then the enemies of Herr von Biener set to work so energetically that, after a short time, they succeeded in turning him out of his position, and imprisoned him on the 28th of August, 1650. A royal commission of noblemen, consisting of Biener's greatest enemies, hastened down to Büchsenhausen, and claimed from his wife all his papers and documents, amongst which they discovered

G

satires, which were most useful to their purpose. He was accused of high-treason, and, as his enemies were both his accusers and judges, he was condemned to death. His wife visited him while he was in prison, and he, who knew himself to be guiltless of any crime, always consoled her with these words :—"There can be no God in Heaven if they are allowed to murder an innocent man."

On the 17th of July, 1651, Herr von Biener was executed in public. The sword which was used on the occasion is still to be seen in the castle of Büchsenhausen. His wife had sent a messenger to the Emperor to pray for a reprieve, which he had granted; but one of Biener's most deadly enemies, President Schmaus, of the Austrian Court, stopped the messenger, and of course the execution ensued.

A few days afterwards, the rascal who had stopped the merciful errand of the Emperor was found dead through the judgment of God. Frau von Biener went raving mad; through the whole house she tore from room to room, crying, "There is no God; there is no God." At last she climbed up the peak behind the Martinswand, and threw herself over a precipice into a deep chasm, out of which she was carried a corpse to Höttingen, where she was buried on the left-hand side of the altar, under a plain tombstone bearing no inscription, and with only a cross cut upon it.

Since her death she has appeared very often as a wandering ghost to a great number of persons, and the inhabitants of the surrounding country have given her the name of the "Bienerweibele" (Biener's Wife). Clad in long black robes, slowly and solemnly she walks along through all the rooms in the castle, passes through firmly locked doors, stops with a woeful look at the bedside of peacefully sleeping people, appears to each proprietor and his wife before their death with wonderful consolation, always foretelling the immediate approach of the "Dreaded Spirit," and never harms those who have never done her any injury. But in the year 1720, it happened that a descendant of one who had been instrumental in her husband's death, who was sleeping in the castle, was found dead in his bed on the following morning, with a most fearfully contorted neck. The ghost appears in a black velvet mantle, and bears on her head a little bonnet, called in the dialect of the country, "Hicrinnen," embroidered with black lace, and on the back of her head a beautiful little golden crown, which is fastened on her hair by the means of a silver pin. People say that in former times the apparition was quite black, but at present it is more grey, and every day she is becoming more light, until at last her unhappy spirit will be redeemed.

THE LENGMOOS WITCHES.

A RICH peasant of Lengstein had a son who had travelled a great deal, and, on returning home, he laughed at the repeating of the rosary, which all the good peasants are in the habit of saying every evening. His mother was very anxious about the profane ideas and behaviour of her son, for he mocked just as much at every other usage of the holy church, which he was pleased to designate as "jokes of the priests."

One day several of his companions were sitting with him at the inn called 'Zu dem Ritter,' and there some one of them recounted that on every

Thursday night hags had been seen dancing, and carrying on their diabolical practices on the Birchboden, which was close by; they were seen arriving on the mountain from all parts, riding on black bricks, and holding there their unholy Sabbath. On hearing this, the rich peasant's son laughed loudly, and said, "Wait, there I will dance with them;" for it was just Thursday evening. His friends advised him not to do so, but, in spite of their warnings, he set off, and they accompanied him up to the Mittelberg, where stands the Kebelschmiede, and where the wild stream of the Finsterbach rushes through a fearful gully. From thence, the young fellow ran singing gaily through the forest to where there is an open spot, called the Birchboden, and where numberless pyramids of porphyry rise to the height of twenty and thirty feet above the ground.

There he saw the frantic witches dancing and jumping together, and performing all sorts of tricks. This pleased the mad young man, and he ran to take part in their unholy dance; but when the huge clock of the magnificent monastery of Lengmoos struck *one*, the Finsterbach foamed wildly up, and the pyramids of porphyry tottered to their very base. This the friends of the peasant, who were waiting for him, saw perfectly well, and a wild storm of wind and hail came suddenly on, so that they were obliged to take refuge in the hut of the Kebel-schmid (Kebelsmith). There they waited until the morning Angelus had rung, at which moment they knew that the hags' power would come to an end, and then they went to the witches' ground. But how terrified were they when they found their wicked comrade transformed into a stone, and fixed firmly into the earth, so that only three-quarters of him could be seen. His stone form still remains on this dreadful spot, and no green—not even an atom of moss—will grow over the head, body, hands, or feet of the " Witch-dancer."

After nightfall no one dares to approach the scene of this terrible retribution, where stands so fearful a warning to all mockers and despisers of religion.

BINDER-HANSL.

In the hamlet of Wälsch'nofen, about ten miles from the village of Völs, lived a certain Binder-Hansl. He was a broom-binder, and, as his name was Hans (or John), they called him the " Binder-Hansl."

He died in the year 1824, and was regretted all over the country, for he was a noted peasant doctor, or " Wonder Doctor," as they called him. Besides curing all sorts of maladies of man and beast, he had a charm against sorcery and witchcraft, and where any suspicious circumstance took place in house or stable, Hans was called, and never failed to help.

One day, in the time of war, the Binder-Hansl went to the village of Botzen, and on the route, near the lane called Kuntersweg, he met the smith of the village of Kartaun, who had been forced by the French troops to carry their big drum, which was very heavy, and when the smith complained very bitterly about it to his friend, Hans said laughingly, "I should send the drum to the devil, and then I should be rid of it." At this the French punished him for his boldness, by forcing him to march with them, carrying at his turn the drum on his back. So he was obliged to carry it up to the Feigenbrücke, near Blumenau; but when he had arrived there, he set the drum on the ground, and said, "By this way I have come, and by this way I will return;" while a Frenchman, who spoke German perfectly well, said, "Churl, take up the drum, or—" and he lunged at him with his naked sword. But the Binder-Hansl laughed at him, and replied, "We shall see;" and at the same moment he stretched out his hand over the Frenchmen, and they became all as motionless as stones.

There he left them standing, and went laughing from the Feigenbrücke, over the steep mountain lane, which is called the "Katzenleiter" (Cat's Ladder). After he had climbed to the summit of the mountain, he shouted, "Be off, fools, now you have seen my power," and making again a sign with his hand, they all came to life, and taking up their drum they ran off, as only Frenchmen can.

THE GOLD-WORM OF THE ALPBACH VALLEY.

NEAR the "Reichen-Felder" (rich fields), behind the valley of Alpbach, is often to be seen, especially on the eve of holy-days, a gold-worm of wonderful brilliancy, which lies there motionless, and wrinkled in such a manner that it looks like a golden chain.

Sometimes this gold-worm has also been seen down in the valley far beneath the Reichen-Felder, even once so far as the banks of the Alpbach, on a spot which is called G'reit. Several times daring people approached the worm, but when they had come near to him they were struck with an uncontrollable terror; and on running to fetch others as witnesses, on their return the worm was no longer to be seen.

The peasants round about say, "Those people had not the grace of putting something sacred upon the worm, and for that reason it disappeared." After all, it is not stated what the worm is, whether it is a treasure-bloom, or a treasure-guardian, of which there are numbers in this rich gold country.

THE GLUNKEZER GIANT.

IN the Volder valley, out of which rises the Glunkezer, and where now stands the sheep Alp, called Tulfein, is a very picturesque mountain meadow, in the middle of which, some centuries ago, a peaceful King had built his palace, in which he lived with his four daughters, of whom each was more beautiful than the other. Round about the palace was a magnificent garden, full of Wonder-Flowers, and large expanses of meadow-lands, upon which tame Alpine animals browsed in large herds, and of these the four daughters of the King were very fond. They went also very often down into the huts of poor herds-people, to whom they did all sorts of charity, and all around they were honoured and reverenced as protecting genii.

This quiet happiness was troubled, and at last destroyed, by the arrival of a wild giant in this

Alpine paradise, who built himself a cavern on the top of the Glunkezer, from whence, during the night, he roared so dreadfully that the mountains trembled, and huge masses of rock rolled down into the valleys. After he had caught sight of the four daughters of the King, he determined to try and gain one of them for his wife; so he decorated his bearskin mantle with enormous new buttons, tore up a fine tree for a walking-stick, passed his long finger-nails a few times through his shaggy beard and hair, and set off down to the Tulfein to pay his addresses. The King's heart trembled with fright as he saw this pretender to the hand of one of his daughters, and replied that his daughters were perfectly free to choose their own husbands, therefore, if one of them would accept him, he should have no opposition to make.

Upon this the giant made himself as small as possible, but that was not very much, and did not bring him in much either, for one after the other of the girls refused him. This enraged the giant out of bounds, and he determined upon the most terrible vengeance, which he did not tarry in executing as quickly as possible. In the following night,

rocks as large as a house rolled down upon the
Tulfein, hurled against the palace, which they
carried along with its inhabitants into the Wild-
See, into whose depth it disappeared, and which
was almost completely filled up with the tumbling
rocks.   The little of its dark waters which is still
left, now bears the name of the "Schwarzenbrunn"
(black spring), and round about it is a " death valley," for nothing will grow there.

After the vengeance of the giant was satiated,
repentance came over him, and he mourned for the
murdered innocent father and daughters; he sat
for whole nights on the borders of the Wild-See,
into which he gazed, and howled and cried so
incessantly, that even the stones had pity on him, for
they became quite soft, and his cavern trembled
and fell to ruin.   At last he bewitched himself and
became a mountain dwarf, while the King's daughters
were transformed into fairies or mermaids, and
appear often on moonlight nights, floating over the
water.   There then sits the small grey dwarf,
stretching longingly his hands towards their light
forms, which however dissolve in mist; the dwarf
then plunges again into the See, with a noise so

great that it seems as though a large rock had fallen into it, and cools in a cold bath the agony of his remorse.

THE WEAVER OF VOMPERBERG.

THE practice of the medical art is even now in the higher parts of the Tyrol rather in a primitive state. Those who are ill send a common messenger down to the doctor, to whom he has to explain all the illnesses of those who have sent him, and, therefore, he has to consult sometimes for twenty or thirty illnesses at a time. The doctor listens to his explanations, and gives to one patient a potion, to another a tisane, to another an unguent, etc., and hands the whole lot to the messenger. Happy it is if, in the confusion of his ideas, the messenger does not change the medicines, but gives to each patient his own. In this manner used the peasant Vögele to cure, who died in 1855, in the hamlet of Matrai, in the Under Wippthal. From early morning till late in the afternoon his farm was overrun with the sick, or their messengers.

But the arts which the weaver of Vomperberg, near the village of Vomp, in the Inn valley, practised were unknown to human doctor, for they were supernatural. It was generally reported that he was in league with the evil one, and eye-witnesses have even certified that the devil once caught him, but that the clever magician managed to slip through his fingers. This weaver, who died in 1845, once sold a herd of pigs to a peasant on the opposite side of the river Inn. The purchaser was driving his pigs over the bridge called Nothholzer-brücke, and, as they arrived in the middle, lo! they all disappeared. All those to whom he recounted this called out, "The weaver is a cunning fellow, he has got the money, and no doubt he has bewitched the pigs back again to his sheds."

In his anger the peasant, after drinking a few bottles of wine, and when his head was rather hot, returned to the hut of the weaver, who was lying on a long plank, warming his feet against the stove. The indignant and half-drunken peasant threw himself upon the man, and, in his anger, tried to drag him out of the hut by his feet, but oh, Heaven! he had scarcely touched the feet, when they both came off in his hands. Trembling with terror and fright, he dropped the feet on the floor and ran off, and has never dared again to say one word about the loss of the pigs.

THE FIERY SENNIN.

OVER the high valley of Alperschon stands a mountain called Gerichtsalp, belonging to the canton of Landeck, of which the judge, for centuries past, has had the right of letting the meadows to all the different parishes of the district; and from time immemorial it has been the privilege of the flock-herds to pasture there also their own animals, together with those of their masters, and then to sell them in the autumn on their own account.

There was at that time upon the Alp a young "Sennin" (or herd-woman), who had among the herd some of her own pigs, of which she took rather too much care, for she cheated the parish to feed them, and gave them goat-milk and the milk from the butter, so that they soon became very fat and round; while the parish pigs she made live upon the thin cheese whey, upon which, of course, they did not thrive. The Sennin was always gay and joking, and sang the nicest songs, and therefore every one liked her for her good temper, and nobody dreamed that she was an alm thief.

A couple of root seekers of the village of Schnaun, the girl's native village, often climbed the Alp, and one day, when busy over their work, they remained there longer than usual, after the Sennin had driven the herd home. They were in the habit of using the empty enclosure in which the pigs were driven to rest in the middle of the day, as a drying-place for their roots, and when they returned home again, late at night, to Schnaun, they heard to their great astonishment that " the pretty young Sennin " had suddenly died, and they stayed a few days in the village to attend her funeral with the rest of the villagers.

Some few days afterwards, they went up again on the mountain to resume their usual business, and it was almost quite dark as they arrived on their favourite spot. As they approached the enclosure, they heard the voice of some one calling the pigs to their feeding-troughs, which they immediately recognized as that of the dead young Sennin, and, as they approached nearer, they saw her in bodily form, carrying a bucket of whey in her hand, and walking about in the enclosure, but red as a fiery furnace. The men stood thunderstruck and gasped with terror, and the spirit called to them, "Yes, sigh for me; here I must burn until my dishonesty is wiped away, even to the last *pfennig ;* " and in saying this she disappeared from their sight, while making a terrific noise, and enveloped in a cloud of sulphurous smoke.

THE SPIRIT OF THE ZIRL USURER.

BENEATH the Solstein, which stands over 9000 feet high, and upon whose summit on certain Thursdays the witches are said to dance, is situated a dreadful chasm, which takes its name from the charming village of Zirl, which lies at the foot of the mountain, and has more the aspect of a little town than

H

an Alpine village. There once lived a wealthy miller, a noted usurer, who amassed no end of unjustly gained money, and, as after his death none of his wealth was restored to those whom he had defrauded, his spirit was condemned to the depths of the chasm, where he suffered indescribable torments, and often during the night his screams have been heard crying, " Help, help me ! "

About twenty years ago, two merry gazelle hunters were walking in the night from the village of Soln, over the Schützensteig, on their way to Hötting, and, as it became very dark, they resolved to pass the night above the Zirl chasm, for fear of falling, in the darkness, over some precipice, or meeting with any other accident. They lighted a large fire, and during the night they heard somebody call out, "Help, help me." The two men immediately thought some one had fallen down the precipice, and one of them shouted, "Have patience, for the night is too dark for us to venture down the gully, but to-morrow we will help you out." In the early dawn they set off to hunt for a track by which to descend the precipice to the rescue of the unfortunate traveller.

On their way they met the shepherd of Soln, and told him of their night's adventure, and, as they recounted it to him, he said, " There you may look in vain, for this call comes not from a lost traveller, but from the wicked miller;" and he then told them all he knew about the wretched money usurer. Many people of Zirl have also heard these frightful screams for help, first in one place and then in another, for the chasm is dreadfully deep and long. In the very depth of it, and at the foot of the Solstein, lies the Graupenloch, where a roaring torrent forms a high cascade, and fills the chasm with the roar of thunder, and even to this day nobody has ever dared to descend to this spot. There sits the spirit of the miserable usurer, howling, with chattering teeth, in his freezing torment.

THE ALPINE HORSE-PHANTOM.

ON the high Alp, called Els, in the Hinderdux, resides a mountain spirit, which the inhabitants of the surrounding country are unable to paint horribly enough. It is described as a terrible horse-phantom, which nobody dare approach, and which snorts fever and death wheresoever it goes. Many mountaineers and gazelle-hunters have met with their death by this spirit, and only he is safe who has gun, sword, and dogs with him.

One day a courageous Alpine hunter resolved to go and fight the mountain ghost, so he loaded his rifle with a crossed bullet, and climbed up the mountain. Not far from the hut, which stands on the Els Alp, is a cross, at which he knelt and repeated a prayer, and he had scarcely left the spot, when a little grey mountain dwarf drew near to him, and begged for a little bread and brandy. The huntsman shared with the dwarf his bread and smoked-gazelle meat; after which the little grey man told him to go back, and bring his gun, sword, and dogs, or else he would be powerless against the mountain ghost, who otherwise would smash him into pieces. The gazelle-hunter followed this advice, and soon returned to execute his courageous purpose.

But it happened far otherwise than he had

expected. The mountain ghost, in the form of a horrible horse, appeared, and galloped upon him with tremendous fury, snorting fire and sulphurous smoke, stamping, and roaring, and neighing so loud, that the very mountain shook with the sound; then he shouted to the huntsman with a voice of thunder, " You rascal, if you had not gun, sword, and dogs with you, I should smash you to pieces."

At this reception, the huntsman stood like one petrified; his teeth chattered, and all desire to fight with a ghost passed away for ever from his mind. The horse-phantom then turned his heels and galloped back again to the Gletscherwand, from whence he had come.

THE WITCHES OF G'STOAG.

NOT many years ago a very rough mountain lane led from Tarenz to Imst, which was called the G'stoag; the post-road now runs over this spot, and still bears the same name.

The tailor, Anton Gurschler, of Strad, once re-

turned home from Grieseck, near Tarenz, where he
had been to visit his sweetheart. It was getting
on for the ghost hour, and as he arrived near the
smith's shop, called Hoada-Schmiede, near G'stoag,
he ran up against a little chapel, which is consecrated to the holy Vitus, and, having hurt himself
in the violence of the shock, he was very angry,
and began to swear, for he wanted to know who
had pushed him so savagely. At that moment a
carriage with lights drove up, and in it were sitting
some women, whom the tailor immediately recognized perfectly well. They stopped the carriage,
alighted, and offered to dance with him, and turned
him round and round, without his being able to
resist them. Then, as they released him, one of
them whispered in his ear, " If you say one word
about this, you had better look out for yourself; "
and then they drove off like a flash of lightning.
The tailor was stupefied with amazement, and, in
his anger, he recounted to his friends at home all
that had befallen him, in which, however, he did
very wrong, for he grew thin and ill, and went out
at last like the spark of a candle.

To another man, a shoemaker of Tarenz, whose

name was Jennewein Lambach, happened the following circumstance :—He was on his way to the castle of Starkenberg, close by his village, and on passing by the church, he neither stopped a moment, nor crossed himself, as it is the custom in the country to do. It was yet dark, for the shoemaker had got up earlier than he was aware of; all at once he heard the sounds of magnificent music, to which he listened for a long time with delighted ears, and then, to his astonishment, he heard the church clock strike midnight. He shuddered with fright, for he knew that something must be wrong, and hurried on as fast as his legs would carry him to Starkenberg, where he was engaged to work; but as there he could find no peace of mind, on account of his strange accident, he returned home again in the afternoon. While he was sitting drinking a glass of wine with the innkeeper Marrand, of Tarenz, a woman of the village entered the room, and said to him mockingly, " The music last night must have pleased you very much, for you listened like a stupid." The shoemaker was struck dumb and could not reply, for it came to his mind that what he had heard in the preceding night had been hags' music, and that that very same woman had been amongst the number of the witches. From that time he shunned the creature as much as possible, but never told any one what had happened to him on that eventful evening. He then bought himself an alarm clock, which he set up close to his bed, so that he never went again too early to his work, and thus by his silence he no doubt escaped the dreadful fate of the poor tailor.

·   ———

THE HEXELER.

In the village of Hall, in the valley of the Inn, close to Innsbruck, lived a man who was a peasant doctor, cattle doctor, and fisherman, in one person ; he was also a noted witch-finder, and, as such, held in terrible dread by all those who had " red eyes." His name was Kolb, but he was generally called the " Hexeler " (hag hunter), or " Hexenkolb."

One day Kolb was engaged fishing in the lake, called Achenthaler-See, when suddenly thunder-clouds as black as ink collected over his head, and on a sign which he made with his hand, a weather hag fell down into the water. The hag seized the side of Kolb's little boat, who, however, beat the rudder down upon her hands, with the intention of drowning her, but she implored him to save her, promising that she would renounce her witchcraft. " As to me," said Kolb, " I will save you if you will give up your wicked trade; but you must hand over to me your sorcery book, so that I shall know all your hellish artifices, and be able to discover their antidotes." After a long dispute, during which the hag was nearly drowned, she gave him a book, in which her most secret charms were written down.

After that incident, Kolb became one of the first " Wonder Doctors " in the Tyrol. When he was asked to cure somebody, the sufferer was compelled to come to him during the night, and it was only on special occasions that he consented to visit the house of the sick. When he was called to the assistance of a bewitched person, he made exactly at midnight the smoke of five different sorts of herbs, and, while they were burning, the bewitched was gently beaten with a martyr-thorn birch, which had also to be cut during the same night, and through which means, at each stripe that was given, the hag who had bewitched the person received the most terrible blow, so that the blood flowed at each stroke. Kolb went on beating in this way, until the hag appeared and took off the charm. But, during the operation, no one was allowed to speak, and the necromancer alone treated with the witch. If any one had spoken but one word, the Hexcler's power would have gone for that night, and all his work would have been useless.

THE CAT-HAGS OF GRIES.

CATS generally take a large share in anything appertaining to witchcraft, and as single apparitions, out of the company of some hag, they are scarcely, if ever, to be seen; though Peter, one of the servants at the farm of Simel, near the village of Gries, once had the misfortune to meet them.

The farmer was an excellent manager, and never allowed any of his servants to be out in the evening after the Angelus had sounded. But Peter had been a volunteer, during the revolution of 1848, and, as such, he considered himself entitled to take more liberty than the others, and to go after hours and pay a visit to his love. One evening, just as he had arranged to carry out this plan, the farmer, who was a member of the parish administration, said, after supper, to his servants, " Now you all go to bed; at two o'clock to-morrow morning I shall call you, for it has been decided by the Council that we must go oftener on patrol round about, to keep on the look out for the Welsh republicans, which are expected in the country, and to shoot them down wherever they appear, for the sake of preserving order and peace."

This command anything but pleased Peter, who, however, apparently obeyed, and went to bed; but soon afterwards he got up very quietly, and thought to himself, " Long before the clock strikes two I shall be back; " and then he crept silently through the stables, and hurried towards the Berghof farm, on the mountain where his sweetheart lived, to bid her good-bye for ever, should it be necessary, in case he fell in the war against the Welsh rebels.

He remained till one o'clock at the Berghof, and
then he set off home, running as fast as ever he
could, and he had arrived already within a distance
of two or three hundred feet of the Simel farm,
when, just over his head, he caught the sound of
suppressed whispering. He looked about, and lo!
all about him, the air and ground was full of cats,
of all colours and shapes, black, white and tri-
coloured, which sprang upon him from every direction. Frightened out of his wits, poor Peter began
to pray and cross himself, when all at once the
tribe of cats disappeared; but this release did not
last long, for when he had reached the farm, he
found the cats sitting in a swarm round the entrance-
door, and they stopped him from getting in, and
against this no praying, no cross-making could avail,
for the cats set up such a terrific noise, that the
poor bewildered fellow lost his senses of hearing
and seeing. He made up his mind, however, to get
into the farm at any risk, and, springing through
the cats, he gained the little door by which he had
gone out; but the door was closed, so he was
forced to knock at the great entrance, where he
was received by the farmer himself, who, after

giving him a good scolding, concluded his sermon in these words:—"There is nothing so fine spun but that it comes always to the sun."*

THE LOCKSMITH OF THE FLIEGERALM.

UNDER the mountain, Fliegeralm, which now belongs to the Baron Steinbach, of Mühlau, used to stand the shop of a locksmith, whose name was Huis. The hut was situated in a most beautiful position, on the edge of a rushing mountain torrent, close to the side of a dense and magnificent forest of fir-trees. The locksmith was an industrious and fearless man, and the report that during the winter a " Kaser-Mandl " (a Tyrolian mountain ghost) walked about, could not deter him from building his house just beneath the Alm ; so he went up in the autumn to fell trees for its construction, about which he set determinedly to work.

* " Es ist nichts so fein gesponnen,
    Es kommt immer an die Sonnen."

The hut was soon finished, and then the locksmith lighted a large fire and commenced his business. One evening, while engaged over his work, he heard footsteps prowling round the hut, and directly afterwards the door was violently shaken, as though it would be forced in. Huis got up, and called out, "Who is there?" and then opening the door, he said, "Well, come in then;" but nobody was to be seen. He went once more to his work, and again heard the same footsteps about the house; so at last, becoming uncomfortable, he determined to retire to rest, in order that he might get up very early in the morning to finish what he was about.

He laid himself down upon a bundle of hay, on which he soon fell asleep; but an hour or two afterwards he was awakened by a most extraordinary noise, and all at once the terrible Alm ghost stood close beside him, and threw himself instantly upon him, like a big butcher's dog, with fiery eyes, and with the fixed intention of tearing his victim to pieces. But the locksmith brought all his gigantic strength to bear upon the ghost, and dealt him a blow, which hurled him to a distance; then, after this victory, he laid down again in another corner of the hut, and slept peacefully until daybreak ; but from that moment he determined never again to pass the night alone in the hut, and so he returned every evening to the valley, carrying his work with him.

He never recounted one single word to any living soul, except his wife, whom he bound down by the strongest vows never to repeat it to any mortal being ; but a woman's confidence is but a stage secret, open to the ears of all who like to listen to it.

THE SALVE-TOAD.

IT is a well-known fact in the Tyrol that the Jordan chapel, which stands on the mountain, called Salve, and which is dedicated to St. John the Baptist, has been founded by a widow, who, out of maternal weakness, had been the cause of encouraging her only son in all sorts of wickedness, which he carried so far as to become the chief of a band of robbers and

cut-throats. Too late, the infatuated woman discovered the crime of which she had been guilty,
and, in deep repentance, sought her son, and, after
following him for many days, found him at last on
the top of the Hohe Salve.

She then tried to persuade him to give himself
up to justice, but he was obdurate; until one night,
in a dream, the ghastly head of St. John the Baptist appeared to him; after which he gave himself
up to the authorities, and his head, with those of all
his companions, was chopped off. The guilty
mother buried all the heads together, on the top of
the mountain, sold all she had, and devoted it to
the erection of the chapel, which is still standing
there.

Other people recount this legend in a different
manner; they say that the brigand had vowed to
make a pilgrimage upon the Hohe Salve, if Heaven
would only assist him to rid himself of his evil
companions, and help him to lead again a good life.
But, after having obtained the assistance of Heaven,
the brigand forgot his vow, and for that reason he
was compelled after his death to crawl up to the
top of the mountain in the form of a toad, and to

enter into the chapel. After a long time, the poor toad succeeded in climbing the mountain, but at the entrance of the chapel there were always people who pushed and kicked him away. At length, however, he succeeded in entering the chapel, and crawled three times round the altar, after which he was instantly changed into the form of a handsome man, who addressed the people who were praying there, telling them of his brigand life and hard penance, and then he suddenly disappeared from their eyes.

THE UNHOLDENHOF.

In the days of Maximilian the First, Emperor of Germany, there was a forester attached to the Court, who was a real " Unhold " (or monster), of almost supernatural bodily strength, and so much so that he was generally regarded as a giant. After the Emperor's death, the forester left the Court with his only son, who was in every degree the image of his father, and went into the parish of

I

Kreith, in which, since that time, fourteen peasants have built their farms, which, for the most part, are all situated on the Middle Mountain, above the rivers Sill and Rutz, between meadows, uplands, and forests. At the bottom of the valley the whirr of a "Säge," *i. e.* a saw-mill, is constantly to be heard, which stands on the bridge over the Klausbach, over which the roads lead on into the Stubeithal.

There a beautiful spring, well protected by a statue of the holy Nepomuk, offers refreshment and rest to the tired traveller, and about half a mile further on, the road divides into two, and the left-hand branch leads off into a charming mountain-path, on each side of which lies a magnificent forest of Alpine firs and pines, and after a quarter of an hour's ascent, one arrives at a rich and thriving farm, which comprises in its possessions an ancient chapel; but with all this it bears a very bad name, and is called the "Unholdenhof" (or monster farm).

It was on this self-same spot that the forester and his son took up their abode, and they became the dread and abomination of the whole surrounding country, for they practised, partly openly and partly in secret, the most manifold iniquities, so that their nature and bearing grew into something demoniacal. As quarrellers very strong, and as enemies dreadfully revengeful, they showed their diabolical nature by the most inhuman deeds, which brought down injury, not only on those against whom their wrath was directed, but also upon their families for centuries. In the heights of the mountains they turned the beds of the torrents, and devastated by this means the most flourishing tracts of land ; on other places, the Unholde set on fire whole mountain-forests, to allow free room for the avalanches to rush down and overwhelm the farms. Through certain means they cut holes and fissures in the rocks, in which, during the summer, quantities of water collected, which froze in the winter, and then in the spring the thawing ice split the rocks, which then rolled down into the valleys, destroying everything before them. Some of these terrific rock-falls prepared by them ensued only some forty or fifty years afterwards.

Through these iniquitous deeds, they gained the dreaded name of Unholde, which has descended

to their abode to the present day; but at last
Heaven's vengeance reached them. An earthquake
threw the forester's house into ruins, wild mountain
torrents tore over it, and thunderbolts set all
around it in a blaze; and by fire and water, with
which they had sinned, father and son perished,
and were condemned to everlasting torments.
Up to the present day, they are to be seen at
nightfall on the mountain, in the form of two fiery
boars.

A better generation has built a new farm upon
the same spot on which the old Unholdenhof used to
stand; but, against their wish and will, the new
house has kept up the old name, which sometimes
changes into that of Starkenhof, because the wicked
foresters were also called "die Starken" (the
strong ones).

The old peasant Hohlenbauer, who still is living
in the village of Mutters, can recount to the
traveller a great deal about the Unholdenhof; and,
among other things, he would tell him how one day
the forester, in his stupidity, sold valuable parch-
ments to a child's-drum maker of Innsbruck, who,
as stupid as he of whom he had bought them,

erased the writing with a stone, and covered little drums with the priceless documents.

THE FIERY BOAR OF KOHLER-STADL.

On the main road from the village of Mutters to the hamlet of Götzens lies a brown wooden hut in the middle of a lovely flowery plain, which is called the " Broat-Wiese " (broad meadow). The road leads through dells and valleys, and in passing through this grand and desolate spot, the traveller is unable to overcome a certain sense of awe, which overhangs this dreaded spot, particularly should he happen to pass that way after the shades of evening have fallen. The hut is an old hay-shed, which has the resemblance of a large dark coffin ; close to this hut stands a little chapel, erected to the memory of a poor traveller, who was frozen to death on that spot, in the year 1815.

This place is decried and avoided, on account of the fearful apparition, which is said to wander

round the spot; and many a one who has tried to
pass that way during the night has been glad to
return safely back again to the village. Close by
lies a dense forest of fir-trees, the rendezvous of
tribes of ravens, which render the surroundings
still more dismal with their ominous croakings. If,
perchance, the traveller hears the cuckoo, he crosses
himself, for it bears in the Tyrol the reputation of
being the devil's own bird, and the evil one himself, the worst of the phantoms, rejoices in adopting
his voice.

There has frequently been seen upon the plain,
close by the hut, which is called the Kohlerstadl, a
fiery wild boar, and many people are of the opinion
that the old monster of the Unholdenhof, of which
has been spoken in the preceding legend, wanders
about there in that form, while others say that this
same fiery boar is a devil's phantom; and there are
numberless people who have seen it.

A rich peasant of Natters, whose name is Klaus
Sinnis, went up one day with his hay-cart to a
meadow-valley, called Götzens-Lufens, and as he
passed by the Kohlerstadl it was already growing
dark, and night was coming on very fast. There

suddenly the fiery boar rushed before his horses, which began to rear and kick, and he was unable to get them on one step further, so that he was compelled to return home with his empty cart.

A herdsman of Götzens was driving his cows home from Mutters, and close by the dreaded spot he met the boar, tearing madly round in a circle. On catching sight of this hideous phantom, the cows set up their tails and rushed wildly off in every direction, so that most of them fell down the precipices and were lost.

Others have seen on the same spot black dogs, and heard unearthly screams and howls which have pierced to their very soul.

THE BUTCHER OF IMST.

IT is not very long since that there lived at Imst a butcher, who was in the habit of catching other people's sheep on the mountain, to alter their marks, and, after leaving them to run for some time among his own herd, either killed or sold them alive.   This clever dodge succeeded very well for some length of time, but at last the butcher died suddenly, and, after his death, such a terrible ghost was seen several times in the house, that the family were obliged to move out of it, until the ghost should be exorcised by the powers of the Holy Church.

The night-watch of Strad was just calling out the twelfth hour, on a pitch dark night, when all at once two Capuchins approached on the road, both of whom carried a burning candle, and one of them bore under his arm a massive volume.   Between them walked the form of the deceased butcher, clad in black, with the high-crowned hat, which he usually wore when alive, pressed tightly down over his eyes, and his arms crossed before him.   The Capuchins signed the night-watch to step on one side, which, in his terror, he was only too glad to do.   Then he saw them all three pass through the village of Strad, and take the post-road to Nassereit, as far as the inn, called 'Zum Dollinger,' into which, however, they did not enter, but turned over the Gurglthal, towards a klamm, or chasm, through which rushes from the lofty Andelsberg the torrent of Klammbach.

To that spot numbers of ghosts from the neighbourhood of Imst have been consigned, and frequently during the stillness of night are heard the dreadful cries of " Help us.   Hoi—hoiiih ! "

MATZ-LAUTER, THE SORCERER
OF BRIXEN.

MATTHIAS LAUTER, generally known under the name of " Matz-Lauter," was born at Brixen, and used to live on a mountain, near Latzfons.   He was everywhere dreaded, for his sorceries surpassed the power of any other man to excel.   There are still many people living in the neighbourhood who knew him, and can tell many curious things concerning him. Matz used to wander about all the country through, because he could never find rest anywhere, and constantly visited the huts of the peasants, who willingly gave him all he asked for, to rid themselves of his company ; and sometimes, out of thanks, he showed them a few of his tricks.

One day, in the common room of a farm belonging to a well-to-do peasant, he made in each of the four corners a different sort of weather at the same moment. In one corner the sun shone, in the second it was dark, and the wind was whistling gloomily ; in the third, soft warm rain was falling ; and in the fourth, a terrific storm of thunder, lightning, and hail was going on. At another time, he forced fowls, which were on the opposite side of the Eisach valley, to fly over to him and lay eggs at his feet, of which he made a present to the farm-people who had been kind to him.

It was generally believed that his art came from the devil, which, however, has been contradicted by the fact that he tormented and dared the old gentleman far more than any one had ever done before, and it is recounted as perfectly certain that once he forced him to clear a way through a forest, through which it was impossible for even a goat to pass, and with such rapidity that he could ride behind on a fast-galloping horse. Another time he forced his Satanic Majesty to catch an enormous mountain oak, which he pitched down to him from a height of four thousand feet.

Matz-Lauter was also much dreaded as a weather-maker, and often boasted that hating mankind, he took pleasure in harming them; and he confessed that only the ringing of consecrated bells had any control over his power, and if round about there had not been the bells of the chapel of St. Anton, near Feldthurns, those of the church of Laien, the enormous clock of the chapel of Latzfons, and the shrill sounds of the belfry of the chapel of St. Peter, a little pilgrimage about two miles from Latzfons, and a mile or so from his own hut, he would long since have reversed the huge mountain, which stands over the village of Latzfons, and buried in its ruins all who lived on or beneath it.

One day Matz-Lauter was found by some hunts-man dead on the mountain, and directly the news spread, every one wanted to climb up and see his body; but it had disappeared, and even now every peasant of the neighbourhood is certain that the devil carried off the body of the sorcerer, after having first claimed his soul.

THE MOUNTAIN GHOST OF THE VIVANNA.

ABOUT six miles from Graun, above the Endkopf, in the dominions of the Frauenpleiss, which ancient legends report as the residence of several fairies, lies the Grauner-Alp, which is also called the Vivanna, and which belongs to the parish of Graun. Jacob Wolf, a huntsman of Graun, ordinarily called "Kob," started one evening, towards the close of the autumn, on a hunting excursion, and climbed up the Vivanna, intending there to pass the night, so that he might be ready to follow the game at an early hour on the following morning. He entered the hut which stands upon the Alp, and after having laid down upon a bundle of dry grass for his night's rest, he heard the door slowly open, and a little old shrunken woman entered, whose attire was very like that of a Sennin, and who seemed to be quite at home there. She lighted a fire, took cream and flour from a little hole in the wall, and set to work to make cakes. As soon as she had finished them, she called out, "Now we are going to eat, and the one down yonder on the grass must be of the party too."

The huntsman was quite frightened and dared not move, but as the little woman called out a second time with her shrill voice, which sounded almost like a command, he picked up his courage, and approached the spot where the old hag was standing. But, oh, terror! at that moment, in the midst of a most fearful noise, there all at once entered through the door a whole tribe of spitting, growling, and miauling cats, pigs and bucks, besides every description of other wild beasts.

The huntsman sprang quickly back into his corner, seized his rifle, which he had fortunately charged with a crossed bullet, and fired right into the middle of the devil's army, which was entirely dispersed in one moment. No more was either to be seen of the old hag, and her cakes stood burning before the fire, and smelling of all sorts of fearful abominations. The huntsman fled from the spot as quickly as ever he could, and rushed down into the valley, giving up all idea of his hunting excursion. But in the morning he found out that, in his hasty retreat, he had left his hunting-sack behind; and so he set off in broad daylight, accompanied by another man, to the scene of his fearful adventure, where they found the sack, with all its contents, bitten and torn to pieces. When recounting this story, Kob always used to say, " The hell company would have served me the same trick, had I not run off as quickly as I did."

— · —

THE OBERLEITNER OF TERENTEN.

AT Terenten, in the Pusterthal, lies a farm which is called the Oberleitner Hof, and its proprietor, who died about twenty years ago, was known in all the surrounding mountains under the name of " the Old Oberleitner."

This old man was a master of the black art, as well as a great huntsman, who delighted in going over the mountains to the wild rocky valley of the Stillupp and Floiten, in pursuit of stone bucks, of which he killed numbers; and he had indeed car-

ried his infatuation so far that there is not one now
to be seen in the whole neighbourhood.

One day he was out with a fellow-huntsman,
quite on the top of the mountain, and all at once he
said to him, " Look there, my wife is just preparing
the dinner, and as she is not in a good temper to-day
we must try and be home in time, or else we shall
catch a scolding."

" But how can that be possible," answered the
other, " since we have more than a day and a half's
journey before we can reach home ? "

" Never mind that," replied the Oberleitner ; and
as the housewife served the dinner, the two huntsmen entered the room at the same moment as all
the farm people. Of course, this never happened in
a natural way ; but how it came to pass no one can
say. Though everybody of the district believes
firmly that it was an example of Oberleitner's
ability.

Upon one of the farm-buildings of the Oberleitner
Hof is still to be seen, up to the present day, an old
roughly-painted picture, which represents an incident
in the life of the former proprietor of the farm.
Oberleitner was working in an adjoining field,

when he caught sight of several fine stags on the distant Alp, called the Eidechsspitze. He ordered his servant to run home and fetch his rifle, but the man laughingly replied, "They will have time to run away a hundred times before you can reach them."

"Oh!" said the Oberleitner, "I have fixed them there surely enough." And, in fact, there they remained upon the same spot until he arrived on the top of the mountain, where he quietly shot them all down, one after the other.

THE TAILOR OF THE ZIROCK-ALM.

For centuries past it has been the custom that on the Brenner Alp a tailor should live, for the purpose of mending the clothes of the teamsters who pass along that deserted road, on their way to or from Italy. Not long since, one of these men who occupied the hut left it to go and set up business in the inn, called 'Schöllerwirthshaus,' about three miles distant from the Brenner post-house. When not otherwise employed, he occupied his time in rolling heavy stones down into the valley below, knocking to pieces the carts of the teamsters, and killing the horses or men, so that the poor fellows were generally forced to stop at the inn, and when on their arrival, they complained or lamented about their misfortune, the tailor sympathized with them, while taking the occasion to cheat them the more in selling them bad cloth, instead of good, and at much higher prices than were to be had at Brixen or Stertzing, saying that the higher they went up the mountain, the shorter was the wood, as they could see on the trees, and so it was the same with his tailor's yard.

This tailor died suddenly, and, as penance for his crimes, he was obliged to walk in ghostly form between the Brenner post-house and the Schöller-wirthshaus, and even as far down as Gossensass, where he practised many a cruel trick, and still made stones roll down upon the road. At last the harm he did was so great that the teamsters found themselves forced to apply to some Capuchins of Stertzing to banish the ghost. The Capuchins

K

ascended the mountain, and banished him for the winter to the Zirock Alp, while for the summer they consigned him to the mountain called Hühnerspielspitze, which is plainly visible from Stertzing, and from whose peak he often cries so loudly that he is to be heard in the whole valley down below, "Ah! is then the last day not yet near? Ah! if only the last day would soon arrive."

The ghost is forced to roll a great number of stones down into the valley, and every one of those stones he is obliged to carry up again on his shoulders. One day an old herdsman placed upon one of these stones a stick, upon which he had cut a cross, and when the ghost found it he threw it on one side and rolled the stone on. When the herdsman found his stick again, several days afterwards, there were five finger-marks burned into it.

THE THREE SISTERS OF FRASTANZ.

To the east of Frastanz, upon the boundaries of Feldkirch, lies a chain of mountains, leading south-wards towards the principality of Lichtenstein, out of which range rise three lofty bare grey jagged mountain peaks, which form the boundary marks of the country, and bear the name of "the Three Sisters," to which are joined the Frastanz Alps.

Towards the end of the last century, a Venediger-Manndl used to come every year into that country, for the purpose of picking up gold, of which large quantities were to be found, especially in the forest valley of Samina, which is situated between the Three Sisters and the Ziegerberg. The Manndl used to fly through the air from Venice, carrying a large jar, which he put under a mountain spring, which threw up gold grains from a subterranean river, and when the jar was full he flew off with it home again. As a proof, he once showed the jar full of gold to some herdsmen, who were pasturing

their cows in the neighbourhood; but they would
not be taken in, and so they crossed themselves and
let the Venetian go, for they knew that he was a
sorcerer, who practised his arts through supernatural power, like all Venediger-Manndl used to
do.

At that time, there lived at Frastanz three
sisters, who upon a great *fête* day, instead of going
to mass, set out very early in the morning to climb
the mountain, for the purpose of gathering strawberries, which grew there in quantities, with the
intention of selling them in the afternoon at Feldkirch.   Upon the mountain they met the Venediger-
Manndl, who indignantly and furiously asked them,
"What are you doing here to-day?"   The girls
were terrified, for their consciences reproached
them for having neglected their duty on such a
great *fête* day, for the sake of gaining a little
money, and they answered, "Nothing, nothing."
Then the sorcerer replied, with a voice towering
with passion, "Well, then, you shall turn into nothing, nothing but bare rocks, without grass or
leaf, without tree or fruit, and beneath you shall be
hidden my golden wealth, which no mortal being

shall ever succeed in finding." At the same moment the three girls were turned into stone, for the sorcerer, in gaining power over them by their crime, redeemed himself, and delivered them in his stead to the evil one.

There still stand the Three Sisters, touching the clouds as three mountain peaks; but the Venetian has never been seen again, and his wealth-stream is said to have been dried up. The Three Sisters look solemnly down upon the upper part of the valley, called Rheinthal, upon Vaduz, and the country of Lichtenstein.

THE ROSE GARDEN OF KING LAURIN.

THE beautiful and charming surroundings of the village of Algund and the castle of Tirol, which stands above it, are still called the " Rose Garden of King Laurin."

Laurin was the name of a King of the dwarfs; he was old and wise, as well as mild and kind, and he had a daughter, who was as amiable and beautiful as a fairy, or "Salige." This lovely Princess wished to have a garden, and begged her father to give her some ground in the light of the sun, for the King lived in a crystal castle, deep in the interior of the mountain, which crowns the old castle of Tirol. The good father granted his daughter's wish, who now set to work to exterminate all weeds and evil plants from the plain which her father had given her, and planted it with all sorts of rose-trees. In this manner her Rosen-Garten became so beautiful, that up to the present day its aspect renders the weary traveller happy, and causes him to forget for the time all pains and griefs, should he have any. So that every one might enjoy the beauties of her garden, she would not have walls, but surrounded it with gold tissue ribbons.

When and how this peaceful and joyous reign came to an end, the legend does not say; but the neighbourhood still remains a "Gottesgarten" (or paradise), although King Laurin and his beautiful daughter are no more to be seen; only the indisputable fact of their former existence lives fresh and green in the memory of all inhabitants of the surrounding country. Close to the village of Tirol, a dwarf is said to be still residing, whose comic name is Burzinigala, or Burzinigele. Another resides upon the mountain called Mutkopf, behind the same village, who chants in moonlight nights the following song to his native meadows :—" I am so grey, I am so old, that I remember thee three times as meadow-land, and three times as forest."*

Some people say that King Laurin on leaving his castle went to fight against giants and dwarfs in the country from Tirol's Rosengarten, down to the charming Lago del Gardo, and towards Verona, where he was ultimately baptized, and became a Christian.

> * " I bin so grau,
> I bin so alt,
> Denk di dreimal als Wies',
> Und dreimal als Wald ! "

THE PETRIFIED LOVERS OF KRAMSACH.

NEAR Kramsach, in the Under-Inn valley, on the spot where the Brandenberg Achenthal commences, lie on the Middle Mountain some small lakes, and above the farms called Mösern and Freundsheim, about three miles above Kramsach, stands another beautiful lake, close beneath the Mooswand mountain, and above the lake is still to be seen the ruin of an old stronghold, called the Guckenbühl. The daughter of the last Baron who resided there was passionately fond of a poor forester, and when the proud and cruel Baron came to hear of the secret rendezvous between his daughter and the huntsman, he ordered him, one pitch-dark night, to be chased out of the castle by the hounds, and, in the hurry of the flight, the poor fellow fell over a rock into the See, and was drowned.

After this act of cruelty and injustice, the poor girl wandered about silent and abstracted, and would neither enter into any amusement, nor take part in any ordinary pursuit of life. One day she went with her maid down to the lake, and, as she looked into its gloomy depths, she saw the dead body of her lover, and, in the frenzy of grief, she threw herself down into the water. The maid ran home recounting this misfortune, and when the wicked Baron, with all his retinue, arrived on the borders of the lake, neither the body of his poor daughter nor that of the forester were to be found. The two lovers had been changed into rocks, both of which rise out of the lake, like little islands ; the one overgrown with ferns and water weeds, and the other bare as a polished piece of granite.

THE GOLD-SEEKER OF THE TENDRES FARM.

BETWEEN Reshen and Nauders lies the Tendres Farm, and the old farmer, who is still living there, recounts the following tale :—

"In my younger days a Venediger-Manndl used to arrive here every year towards the autumn, dressed in dreadfully ragged black clothes, just like a beggar, who always passed the night in my farm, and left on the following morning in the direction of the Green Lake, towards the Swiss frontier, and returned here again in the evening.

"As I could never comprehend what the little beggar was doing here every year, and as in the same day he could neither reach huts nor farms, where he could get something by begging, I followed him one day, and found him on the borders of the Green Lake, close to a fountain, busily occupied in taking sand out of a wooden trough, into which the spring was running, and putting it into his sack.

"I thought to myself, 'Wait, my little fellow, I will lighten that work for you, and empty the trough before you return again; if the sand is of some value, I also can make some use of it, and if it were of no value, you certainly would never come here from so far to fetch it.' In the following year, towards the autumn, I went to the spring, removed the stone slab from the trough, and found it full of gold sand, which was very heavy. I set off with it directly to Venice, to offer it for sale to a

rich merchant, who was astonished at the sight of
the sand, and said, ' Oh ! you rich man, I have not
money enough to buy all that gold; but go down
into that street, and you will find a large house
shut up ; knock at the door, and the richest man
of Venice will let you in, and buy the treasure
of you.'

"As I approached the house, a distant voice
shouted to me out of one of the windows, ''Tendres
Farmer, bring here your gold.' I could not make
out who could know me, far as I was from my own
country, and, as I entered the palace, I was dazzled
with the magnificence and riches which everywhere
met my eyes. In a splendid chamber, on an arm-
chair of pure gold, was sitting the little beggar,
who had so often passed the night in my farm. He
arose as I entered, and, shaking his finger menac-
ingly at me, said, ' You have not acted honestly in
clearing out my trough ; but, since you have so
often sheltered and fed me, I will give you a day's
pay for the gold, which is my own.' Then he gave
me a gold coin for each day I had been on my
journey, after which he held a glass before my eyes,
in which I saw Tendres, my wife and children

working in the field; in one word, everything as clearly as though I was myself standing in the farm. Then he turned the glass, and I saw the well on the Green Lake with the gold trough, and, after having passed his hand over the glass, he said, 'Now go home, and you will never again find fountain or trough.'

"And so it happened indeed, for when I reached home, and went down to the Green Lake, it was impossible for me to discover one single trace of the Gold Spring."

THE FAIRY OF THE SONNEN-WENDJOCH.

At the foot of the gigantic mountain peak on which stands the Sonnenwendjoch, a chalk Alp, over 8000 feet high, stand the hamlets of Brixlegg, Mehrn, and Zimmermoos, upon a lovely plain, from which the Achen rushes down into the valley, and works the lead, silver, and tin foundries, which are the most important of the whole Tyrol. On that spot a fairy used to reside.

Close by lies the little town of Rattenberg, above which used to stand a magnificent stronghold, of which there are now but a few picturesque ruins to be seen. One day the young Baron of the little castle of Mehrn went hunting upon the charming green mountain side, and as in the pursuit of his game he had approached the Sonnenwendjoch, he caught sight of the fairy of the mountain. To see her and fall deeply in love with her was the work of a moment, and the fairy also returned his affection, for the handsome young Baron pleased her. The fairy, who was a guardian of Alpine animals, ordered the youth never to pursue one of them again if he wished her to take any notice of him. Then she led him into her dominions, in which there were endless magnificent things to be seen—gardens of never-fading flowers; deep, clear fountains; meadows, upon which animals were peacefully browsing; and grottoes supported by crystal columns, and whose roofs and walls were like mirrors. They then became engaged, and the Baron received from the fairy a ring as gage of her favour

After that he often went out under the pretence
of hunting, but never brought home any game; at
which every one was astonished, because he was
noted as a good shot and clever huntsman, and
had already killed many bears and boars with his
dagger alone. Every one was surprised, too, to see
that he avoided all the surrounding castles, and
seemed to have made up his mind to remain un-
married. Meanwhile, it happened that in the castle
of Rattenberg a wedding took place, to which the
lord also invited his friend the Baron of Mehrn;
and, as it was impossible for him to decline this
invitation, he attended the wedding to his great
grief, for there he met a young lady of Innsbruck
who entangled him in her toils, and pleased him so
much that he gave her the fairy's ring which she
had noticed glittering on his finger.

Overcome by shame and remorse at his infidelity,
he went on the following morning to the Sonnenwendjoch, where he saw a white doe bounding
before him. At that sight the old love of hunting
awoke in him, and he pursued the animal to a
well-known spot, where, by knocking with his ring,
a door in the rock sprang open which led to the

entrance of the fairy's empire. There the youth stood rooted to the ground with terror, for he had not the ring; and suddenly the fairy herself appeared before him, dignified and haughty, not in anger, but in deep grief. She held the ring in her delicate hand, and said in a low sad voice: "You are unfaithful. You have sworn always to think but of me; never to give my ring to another; never to pursue one of my animals, and you have thrice broken your oath. Farewell!"—and in saying so she disappeared from before his eyes.

The Baron had scarcely left the spot when a huge rock rolled down the mountain with the noise of thunder and covered a large portion of the valley with its *débris*. After that the young man became sad and dejected and left the country, and people say that he went to the Holy Land, from which he has never returned.

THE FIREMAN PIGERPÜTZ.

At the foot of the Ischürgant mountain, near Imsh, stands a stone hut, called the Hirnhutte, because it had been erected by a former wood merchant whose name was Hirn, as a resting-place for his woodmen when he was felling timber on the banks of the torrent Pigersbach. This place is regarded with horror on account of a terrible shade which wanders from the Pigersbach upwards through an immense forest of gigantic oaks, and then passes over Strad up to the dense forest of firs which lies beyond.

This apparition, which is generally called the Pigerpütz, appears as a headless black form, or tears through the air in the shape of a flame which is sometimes larger and sometimes smaller, sometimes lighter and sometimes darker, and which often has been seen to rise above the ground expanding as it goes to the height of sixty feet and more.

In the year 1849 it happened that four peasants

set out during the night from Imst to Tarenz, and
as they walked along the Pigersbach which flowed
on their right through mossy plains, they saw a
brilliant flame floating across their path. " There
goes the Pigerpütz," said one of the men, and the
others who were a little hot from the wine which
they had taken at Imst, began to laugh and sneer at
him ; but they had scarcely done so ere the flame
rushed upon them, and as they saw this the three
tipsy men ran off as fast as their legs could carry
them, but the one who had first seen and spoken of
the Pigerpütz stood firmly on the spot. He was the
peasant banker of Tarenz, who is still alive and
recounts his adventure thus :—

" I stood firm and let him approach, and, by my
soul, he really came on and grew to the size of a
haystack as he approached. Then I said to him :
' I shall never help you; for if you had led a better
life, and not committed so many crimes, you would
not now be obliged to wander about in this form.
Now off with you ! ' And then, by my soul, he
really fled away over the Pigersbach."

THE PILLER-SEE.

WHERE the lovely Piller-See now lies, with its green rippling waters about one and a half miles long by three-quarters wide, close to the village of St. Ulrich, there used to stand one of the most beautiful and most fertile Alps of the whole Tyrol, belonging formerly to several peasants, who pastured large herds of animals upon it. They were rich in cows, and grass, and had their beautiful Alp besides to depend upon; so they were the happiest and wealthiest peasants in all the world. But instead of being grateful to Heaven for all its blessings, they became vain, thinking only of amusement and dancing, and every Sunday and fête-day they passed in all sorts of frivolous pleasures. The Alp soon assumed the appearance of a heathen garden, and all those who paid no regard to the opinion of the world flocked there to enjoy their guilty pleasure.

The dissolute villagers wanting one day to play at their favourite game of ninepins, and having neither balls nor pins, seized upon the beautiful alpine which they found in a farm close by, ready for the morrow's market, and turned it to the purposes of their game; but suddenly the shed in which they were amusing themselves began to give way, and all the surrounding ground, together with the adjacent mountains, sank beneath their feet. Upon whatever spot they trod the earth slipped from under them, and out of the earth water sprang, and every one of them was drowned in the new-formed lake. Only a musician who had been forced against his will to climb the Alp and play to them was saved, for, sitting on his chair, he was driven to the borders of the lake by the swelling current.

This lake is now called the " Piller-See," which in certain places is fathomless. One day some people tried to measure its depth, when they heard a hollow voice proceeding from the bottom of the See, calling out :—

"If you fathom me, I swallow you."*

This, like many other of the Tyrolian lakes, is

* Ergründest Du mich,
  So verschling' ich Dich.

supposed to have the power of dragging into its fathomless depths all those who are unfortunate enough to fall asleep on its fatal shores.

THE BURNING PINES.

A POOR widow of Rattenberg, who was blessed with a large family, had been, through endless misfortunes, reduced to such a pitch of poverty that she only had left of all her possessions a small wood in the valley of Scheibenthal, which is close to Rattenberg. A wicked-hearted wretch took advantage of her troubles to try and prove that the wood was his own property, and by means of false witnesses and many failures of justice matters were driven so far that the unfortunate widow had to give up the wood, and died of grief soon afterwards. The children were taken care of by good neighbours, and when they were strong enough they were obliged to go out to service, and soon no more was heard of the matter.

Everything would have been forgotten had there

not been One in whose remembrance all lives;
and up to the present day the crime of the forest
thief is constantly recalled through the circumstance that burning trunks often roll down through
the wood, sending sparks in all directions, sometimes assuming the terrific appearance of a forest
fire. But this dreadful phenomenon is ascribed to
the fact that the wicked man, with his vile companions who had robbed the poor widow of her
wood, have been condemned to burn in the forest
which they stole, under the form of fiery pines, and
roll in their agony through the forest, vainly seeking to release themselves from their everlasting
punishment.

THE JAUFEN-FAIRY.

UNDER the summit of the Jaufen, a mountain in
Passeier, about 8000 feet high, used to reside a
fairy who fell passionately in love with a young
Baron of the castle of Jaufenburg, which lies
at the foot of the aforesaid mountain, and was

formerly the residence of the lords of Passeier.
But whether the heart of the Baron was no longer
free, or whether the fairy's love frightened him,
cannot be said; but he never responded to the
attention of his fairy admirer, who took his cool-
ness so much to heart that she pined away and
transformed herself into a beggar woman, in which
form she wandered along all the lanes and passes
through which the Baron generally took his way,
the image of injury and grief. One day she hid
herself in a chalk-burner's hut at which the Baron
often stopped, as the man had been his former servant. When the young nobleman arrived and
asked for a draught of water, the transformed fairy
brought it to him after having dropped a pearl into
the glass. While the Baron drank, the fairy assumed her real form, and now she appeared to him
most beautiful, for the pearl had bewitched the
water so that it coursed through his whole frame
like fire, inspiring him with a never-before-felt
sensation. The beautiful cup-server who stood
before him seemed the acme of his ideal. He set
her before him on his charger and galloped off to
the Jaufenburg.

But a wonderful thing came to pass; his beautiful bride suddenly disappeared from his side, and he could not imagine where she had gone. He rode day and night and never reached his castle. The poor exhausted charger at last fell beneath the weight of his infatuated master, and died. Then the Baron sought his home on foot, but without avail; he found himself in a strange country where he knew nobody and nobody knew him. He became so poor that he was obliged to sell his rich attire, and at last was forced to beg his way through the country. Miserable, weak, and ill, he reached one evening the hut of the smith in the Kalmthal, where, half dead with hunger and exposure, he fell down upon a heap of straw.

The fairy now saw good to bring to an end the hard penance which she had imposed upon him for his first slighting of her. She appeared to him again in all her grace and splendour. All his magnificent attire was restored to him; his charger stood waiting for him at the door of the hut, and all the hardship through which he had passed appeared to him but as a dreadful dream. He now conducted his fairy bride back to the Jaufenburg, united himself to her for ever, and lived happy and blessed, though without any heir. After his death the fairy disappeared, and the Jaufenburg descended by marriage to the family Von Fuchs, and, later on, the beautiful castle fell into the hands of a rich peasant and crumbled to ruins under his keeping.

THE WETTER-SEE.

CLOSE beneath the mountain Gerlos, in the Zillerthal, lies the "Wetter-See" (weather-lake), into which no one dares to throw a stone, and it is not advisable for even a stranger to do so, or he would find himself involved in great trouble from the surrounding mountaineers, among whom still exists the firm belief, which has been corroborated by hundreds of examples, that directly a stone has been thrown into the lake fearful thunderstorms arise, accompanied by devastating hail and wind.

The See lies in a desolate basin on the heights of the mountains, and every one who is shown the lake hears from his guide, or any cowherd, the following legend : A shepherd arrived one day on the borders of the See, where he saw a huge golden chain lying, the other end of which remained in the water. Just as he stooped to grasp it he saw, glittering on the other side of the lake, one of much larger size, so he left the first to go and take the other; but as he approached it and was about to put his hand upon it, both chains disappeared under the water, while the poor fellow stood stupefied with amazement on the shore.

People say that "the herdsman was too avaricious; for, had he been content with the one chain which was within his grasp, he would never have lost them both." As the chains are said to appear from time to time, people are still on the look-out for them, because they are of such enormous length that he who finds one of them would be rich during all his days.

THE COURAGEOUS SERVANT GIRL
OF THE ZOTTA-FARM.

In the Wattenserthal, which is about twenty miles
in length, and where at its end the Hochlizum
Alp stands, lies on the right of the mountain
the beautiful Wotz Mountain, belonging to the
farmer of Zotta-Hof, which stands at its foot.
Upon that mountain, during the winter time, a
" Kaser-Manndl " (a sort of ghost) is said to reside.
This spirit inhabits a hut which is situated on the
top of the mountain, from whence he makes a
terrific noise, which is heard for miles around; but
towards Christmas he becomes more quiet and goes
off again in the spring. Before his departure a
blackbird sings during many days, from a pine
which stands on the mountain, so beautifully that
one could listen to her for hours together.

Now it happened that in the house of the Zotta
peasant a poor servant girl was employed whose
mother was very ill. As Christmas Day approached

she had to clean up the whole house, and on the Eve
the farmer divided the Christmas-cake between his
family and servants; and while he enjoyed his portion in company with his friends and neighbours,
one of them asked: "What is the Kaser-Manndl
about to-day? I wonder whether he is fêting Christmas as well?" The farmer, who had been drinking
considerably, shouted in good humour: "I will give
the best cow out of my herd to whomever has the
courage to go up the mountain to-night and find
out what the Kaser-Manndl is doing, and brings me
back in proof his milking-bucket and foot-warmer."

But all heard this proposition in silence, for none
of them dared risk so much danger to gain the cow,
because the Kaser-Manndl was noted for his ferocity, and many a one had returned from his neighbourhood with a head almost smashed to pieces.
But the poor servant girl collected her courage and
thought to herself: "I will undertake it in God's
name. Should I gain the cow, I shall be able to
help my poor sick mother, and as I have not the
intention of going out of curiosity, Heaven will
protect me." So she agreed with the Zotta farmer,
and set off up the Alp, which is a constant ascent

of six miles, battling with bitter wind and snow as she went.

Far above her she saw the Kaser, or, hut, brilliantly lighted. Everything in it was clean to perfection, and the Kaser-Manndl was sitting in his Sunday clothes at the hearth, his nose-warmer smoked in his mouth, and he was cooking in a pan a coal-black meal. On entering the hut the girl made as fine a curtsey as a peasant girl is able to do, and the Manndl signed to her to approach the fire and join him at his supper; but the girl was terrified at the sight of the compound, and when the Manndl noticed this he said, "Do not be frightened, girl; make only a 'Krizl Krazl' (a sign of the Cross) over the pan." The girl did this, and to her great astonishment the pan became full of the most beautiful cakes, which they both set to work to eat.

After a little while the Kaser-Manndl said, "I know the request you wish to ask. You have come to carry off my milking-bucket and foot-warmer. You shall have them without the asking, for you are a brave girl, and when you arrive at the farm you will claim of the peasant his cow together with the calf as punishment for having allowed you to come up in such fearful weather."

The Zotta peasant was just setting out for the midnight mass as his servant returned from the Alp with her proofs, and when she claimed the cow he called her a stupid fool for having gone up the Alp and taken his joke as reality, and he would not give her one *pfennig*, much less the cow.

On the following morning there was a grievous Christmas-gift at the Zotta-Hof: the Robblerin, the finest cow, lay dead in the stable, and the farmer nearly tore off all his hair with grief, for this cow had been his favourite and had carried the first prize at every show, for which reason he had given her the name of ".Robblerin," or champion. " Had you given the cow to me," said the poor injured girl to her master, " she would not have died. Will you now keep your word and give me another?" But the farmer savagely refused this demand.

On the following morning they found that another beautiful cow, named " Maierin," had strangled herself with her chain. On the next day a third cow was found dead, and only now the peasant's hard heart began to melt, for he was fearful lest he might lose his whole herd, and therefore he gave the finest remaining cow to the girl, who directly drove her off home; and from that moment poverty came to an end in the house of the courageous servant girl, who prayed day and night for the redemption of the Kaser-Manndl of the Wotz-Alm.

THE KLAUSENMANN ON THE KUMMER-SEE.

In the Hinder Passeier lies the village of Moos, about which, on account of the frequent accidents that there take place by people falling over the adjacent precipice, the following saying is common in the Tyrol: "At Moos even cats and vultures break their necks."*

In 1401 a part of the mountain standing about a mile from the village fell down into the valley, buried the farm called Erlhof under its *débris*, and caused the water running through the valley to

* Zu Moos zerschellen selbst die Katzen und Geier.

collect and form a large " see," or lake, which
through its inundations created so much *Kummer*
or grief in the valley that it received from the
inhabitants the name of "Kummer-See" (Lake of
grief).

The legend goes that after the mountain by the
will of God had been cloven, and the Kummer-See
formed by the power of the Evil One, a " Klausenmann," or sluiceman, was set there to look after the
lake, and warn the neighbours in time, were it
impossible to let the water off. But for this work
a pious man was needed, whose prayers alone would
keep the swelling waters within bounds ; for the
devil used to bathe in the lake, and made such a
fearful noise that he could be heard even as far
down as Moos. The villagers made frequent pilgrimages for the purpose of being preserved from
the calamities caused by this dreaded See ; but as
after a time they omitted this practice, the most
fearful inundations ensued, leaving everywhere behind them ruin and desolation.

The Klausenmann, too, became so corrupted that
he forgot all his religious duties, never went to
church, and always worked on Sundays and fête-

days; so the Demon of Evil once more gained
power and there was another terrific inundation
which transformed the whole Passeier-Thal into a
vast ocean, entered into the Etsch-Thal, and destroyed a great part of the village of Meran.   In
this flood the wicked Klausenmann perished, and
after his death his wretched spirit was consigned
to wander about on the shores of the See, which
has since dried up, and in its place now stands a
desolate swamp.

The modern traveller meets on his road round
the former site of the See, a rock called z' Gsteig,
upon which pious hands have erected a chapel.
There, as evening falls, fearful groans are often to
be heard, while the terrible shade of the Klausenmann rushes by the sacred spot.

THE VILLAGE ON THE BODEN-
ALP.

AFTER traversing the valley of the Almajur, which
sends its waters into the river Lech, one arrives at

the Boden-Alp, which, together with the mountain called Almajur, belongs to the village of Stanz. Upon the Almplace of the Boden used to stand in days gone by a beautiful village which had become, through the neighbouring silver mines belonging to it, immensely rich. The inhabitants in course of time grew so luxurious that they did not know what to do with their wealth, and it came into their heads to fill their houses with all sorts of utensils of gold and silver. They even kept their windows shut during the day, for the light of God's beautiful sun was not good enough for them, and preferred in their iniquity to burn candles in massive silver candlesticks. The patience of Heaven regarded this crime for very long, hoping, perhaps, that the folly would outwork itself; but as it only increased the more, the Lord proceeded with his just punishment. The whole village with its church and people sank beneath the earth, and the once flourishing valley became a desolate wilderness.

About forty years ago a herdboy of Boden went about in the underwood seeking for a lost calf, when all of a sudden he ran up against a large iron cross which was standing out from the ground.

M

This was the cross on the tower of the sunken church. He tried to drag it up and cleared away the surrounding bushes; there he discovered the coping stones of the tower, on which the cross was so firmly planted that he could not move it; and when he returned on the following day with several other people to dig it out, it was no longer to be seen.

Not many years ago a peasant of Hegerau in the Lech-Thal, whose name was Klotz, passed by that mountain and entered into a sort of tunnel through the rock, where, on account of the bad weather, he took shelter. He lighted a torch to discover the depth of the tunnel, and in walking on he suddenly found himself in the sunken church. The high altar was gorgeously lighted, and the candles stood in large silver lustres. The peasant walked about in the church, and found a man sleeping on one of the benches, who as he awoke him inquired the time, and when the peasant told him, he sighed and said, " Ah ! it is still far from the time."

What he meant by these words remains still an enigma, but the peasant seized one of the silver lustres from the altar and ran off in terror. He arrived home late at night carrying the lustre, and would have believed all as a dreadful dream, had he not the lustre with him as witness. He went to rest, and on the following morning he was dead. His wife ordered the lustre to be carried back to its place, but it was impossible to find again the entrance of the underground church.

THE GOLD-MEASURERS OF LOFER.

In Lofer, a hamlet on the Tyrolian frontier towards Salzburg, lived a rich peasant who on his death left behind him three daughters, of whom the youngest was totally blind. The mother was long since dead, and so, after the demise of their father, the three orphans set about dividing the money and property which he had left to them. They found so large a treasure in the old man's coffers that they were obliged to divide it by means of a sieve, by which the two eldest girls shamefully took advantage of the infirmity of their poor sister to cheat her of her share. Each time the blind sister's turn came round they reversed the sieve and covered only the bottom with money, so that the poor deluded girl in placing her hand upon it should be convinced that she received her right share.

In this way, of course, she never got even a hundredth part of what was her due, and after the division was finished the avaricious sisters hid their unjustly gained wealth in a secret hole in a rock on the mountain. But the All-seeing Eye of Heaven remains ever open, and on the death of the two sisters they were condemned to lie in the form of black ferocious dogs in the cavern and to guard their hidden and ill-gotten treasure. There they are chained until their unholy wealth is exhausted by those who succeed in approaching it and take of it only so much as they really want; for all who attempt to carry off more are immediately seized upon by the infuriated guardians and torn into atoms. But as there are few in the world who are contented with real necessities, the treacherous sisters will doubtless be compelled to sit over their unjustly-gained wealth for many ages to come.

THE ANTHOLZER-SEE.

WHERE now lies the beautiful lake in the Puster-Thal with its rippling green waters, three magnificent farms used to stand surrounded by expanses of rich and fertile ground.

One year, when the Kermesse was being celebrated, on which day every one indulges in something more than usual, an old beggar man arrived in each of the farms and asked for charity, begging even for any dry morsels that remained from their meal. But the peasants were one and all selfish and avaricious, and so they kicked the poor mendicant from the door. The beggar then said in anger to each of them: "Take care! in three days a spring shall rise behind your farm, and then your eyes will open; so look to what will happen!"

The peasants, however, cared little for the beggar's threat, and laughed at him; but on the third day a spring arose behind each farm, and their united waters increased to such an extent that they soon formed a lake which devoured in its depth the farms and their inhabitants.

This is the Antholzer-See, also called Spitaler Hochsee, which now stands surrounded by dark forests of gigantic pines.

THE MAILED GHOST OF BRIXEN CASTLE.

At Brixen still stands the magnificent ancestral castle of the Lords von Lachmüller—one of the most ancient families of the Tyrolian nobility. In the old picture gallery of this deserted mansion, the ghost of one of the knights whose portraits still hang there, wanders about.

During the time of the French invasion in 1797, a French officer was quartered in the castle with several soldiers. On account of the numerous family of the proprietor, there were but a few small chambers vacant in the building, and as the officer was not contented with the room which had been allotted to him, he roughly demanded one larger and with finer site. But there was only the picture gallery left, in which the officer took up his abode, laughing and sneering at the warnings given him by the host that the corridor was said to be haunted. The strong-headed fellow took every precaution to guard himself against either natural or supernatural apparition, and after he had ordered a strong trooper to lie down close beside him, he went to sleep devoid of any fear.

But, as he awoke at midnight, he saw a knight in full attire standing before him, who regarded him most ferociously. The officer shouted at him, but, as he stood his ground and paid no heed, he transfixed the form with his long sharp sword, which lay unsheathed beside him. At this instant, the apparition stretched out his arms, seized the officer, and hugged him so closely and long, that he lost his breath.

The trooper awoke late in the morning, and, on finding his master dying, he summoned all the inhabitants of the castle, to whom the officer, who came to himself again, recounted in a feeble voice what had happened to him, and pointed out one of the ancestral portraits as the being who had ap-

peared before his bed and hugged him so fearfully.
Two hours afterwards he died.

THE TREASURE OF THE
SIGMUNDSBURG.

At the foot of the Fern Alp, about two miles from
Nassereit, lies a small deep green Alpine See, and
on a rock, which overhangs it, stands the old
castle of Sigmundsburg.   Beneath the walls of the
castle are deep vaults, hewn in the solid rock, in
which is buried an incalculable treasure, whose
guardian has the form of a big hairy black dog.
Sometimes, too, the dog appears like a luminous
mass, without, however, burning; in his mouth he
holds a key, which opens the door of the treasure-
room, but the conditions on which the treasure can
be got at are unknown to any one.   Besides, the
cellar is so well guarded that it is very difficult to
approach it; and people say that most probably
the Sigmundsburg must fall into ruins before the
cellar can be entered, and then only the treasure-

guardian may have the chance of finding the re-
demptor, for whom he is already so long waiting;
but before that moment arrives, two centuries will
perhaps still have to elapse.

THE FRATRICIDE UPON THE HOCHALP.

THE "Hochalp" (or High Alp), near Scharnitz,
was some two centuries ago covered up to the top
with the finest grass and woods, and the now
cleared Fitzwald was the most beautiful forest in
the whole Tyrol. It reached up to the very summit of the mountain, which was covered with such
enormous trees, that three men could not encom-
pass one of them with their arms; in one word, the
Hochalp was a " Cow-Heaven," as it was generally
called by the peasants. Where now the sheep
climb about, at that time there were but cows
pastured, and the cattle thrived there better than
anywhere else.

The Alp belonged to a rich peasant of Leutasch,

named Simele, who had two sons, who, after his death, commenced a serious quarrel about which of them was to have the Alp. The younger brother was a good man, but the other was a real wretch; and, as they could not agree, they drew lots for the Alp, which fell to Johann, the younger of the two.

After this he married a good village girl, whom his brother Matz had set his eyes upon, and from whom he had received a refusal. Johann lived happily with his wife, while his brother boiled over with bitter spite, and month after month his determination of seeking revenge increased. He commenced a law suit, finding false witnesses, and swore a false oath, so that the Court declared the drawing invalid, and awarded the Alp to Matz.

Whilst all this was going on, Johann was busy on the Alp, and so heard nothing of the judgment; and as his brother entered fiercely into the hut, and tried to pitch him out of it, he defended himself until his herdsmen arrived, who chased him away, after having beaten him soundly. At this reception Matz foamed with rage; so, running home, he seized his gun, crept in the following night back to the hut in which his brother was sleeping, and shot him dead in his bed.

But Johann's soul was scarcely out of his body, when God's wrath appeared and fearfully punished the perjurer and fratricide. A terrible storm came on with lightning, thunder, snow, hail, and wild pouring rains, so that everything was overthrown and inundated. After that an earthquake convulsed the ground, and on both sides the mountains fell into the valley, covering the Alm huts and meadows more than sixty feet deep with *débris*. The murderer was swallowed among the falling rocks, and is condemned to suffer dreadfully beneath them. He is still heard very often shrieking in agony, and all the pilgrimages which his family have made for his redemption have been in vain.

As nobody could do anything with the valley covered with rocks and stones, the decried spot fell into the hands of the monastery of Werdenfels, and wherever it was possible, the monks have restored cultivation, so that new forests and meadows have in course of time sprung up upon the ruins of the once famous Alp.

A beautiful little chapel has been erected there, in which several times during the course of the year service is performed; but the spirit of the murderer still wanders around and groans so dreadfully during the night, that every one is terrified. There he must remain until the last day, and what will happen to him then God alone knows.

THE TWO HAYSTACKS.

ONE of the most beautiful and noted Alps in the Tyrol is the Seisser-Alp, in the Eisack valley, not far from which stands the Schlern, 8100 feet high, with its two pyramids of dolomite rock. About four miles from the Schlern, and joining the wonderful Rosen Garten of King Laurin, are the Rothe Wand and the Rothe Wies, out of which rise two enormous peaks.

Upon the Schlern pilgrims resort to the Holy Cassian, and on the day of this Saint, the fifth of August, there takes place every year a great *fête* in the chapel, which stands on the spot. From the parish of Völs, which lies about nine miles lower down, the inhabitants wend on that day up the mountain to the chapel, and all the mountaineers from the Seisser-Alp assemble there in their Sunday's best to *fête* the Saint.

One day it came into the mind of a farmer to make hay on St. Cassian's day. His servant reluctantly obeyed his commands, and his neighbours kind-heartedly warned him that it was a crime to make hay on the day of the Saint who was so universally revered. But the farmer laughed mockingly, and said, " Be it Cassian's day or not, the hay must up upon the stacks ; "* and so he worked on the faster with his servants. At last all the hay, after having been raked together, was pitched up in two large heaps, which are called there, " Schober," and as the last forkful was thrown upon the top, the two " Heuschober " (haystacks) were turned into stone, and in this shape they still stand on the same spot as an everlasting warning. Since that time no one has ever again thought of working on St. Cassian's day.

* " Cassiantag hin, Cassiantag her,
    'S Heu muss in die Schober ! "

THE SUNKEN FORESTS.

NEAR the village of Kitzbühel used to stand a magnificent forest, about which two peasants had a lawsuit of several years' duration, which finished with the judge being corrupted by one of the two peasants, to whom he awarded the Alp, and sent the defendant off, without the least hope of ever regaining his right.

The losing party, who through this iniquitous proceeding had become a poor man, could not rest, and constantly bewailed his misfortune, saying that he had been cheated and unjustly condemned. But the other, hearing the constant complaining of the poor injured man, one day called out, " Well, then, by all the devils, keep on crying. If I have unlawfully gained the forest, may it sink three thousand feet beneath the ground." These words had scarcely gone out of his mouth, when an earthquake took place, together with a fearful thunderstorm, and the majestic forest sank beneath his feet, and black waves directly rolled over it.

Though enormously deep as the See is, during certain weather the forms of trees can be distinctly seen far down below.

The same is the case with the Lanser-See, upon whose bottom trees are also to be seen growing. Where now this See stands, there used to be a magnificent forest of pines, about which, too, a dispute took place, though not between two peasants, but between a peasant and a nobleman, and the trial was conducted in such a manner that the nobleman gained the forest away from the poor man, to whom it really belonged; for, according to the old Tyrolian saying, "Noblemen do not bite each other."* But the poor peasant, in his anger, cursed the forest, root and branch, and it sank into the depths of the earth. Next morning it was no longer to be seen, but a deep See stood in its place, which, after the village of Lans, not far from the renowned castle of Ambras, has taken the name of Lanser-See.

* "Die Edelleute beissen einander nicht."

TANNEN-EH'.

HIGH up in the Tyrolian Alps formerly stood a fine city, called Tannen-Eh', whose inhabitants for ages past had led honest and God-fearing lives. There used to be a Paradise of peace and happiness; no one ever thought of hunting or killing any game; domestic animals, and Alpine plants and fruits being sufficient for the wants of the good-hearted simple people. There were never quarrels or disputes about "mine or thine," the rich man willingly helped his poorer neighbour, and there was no extremity of wealth or poverty at Tannen-Eh'.

But in course of time all was altered. With increasing wealth the lust of gain approached, which brought vanity and luxury in its train. They said, like the people of Babel, "Let us build a tower whose top shall reach the skies, so as to gain ourselves a name, and in the tower there shall be a bell, whose sound can be heard by all those who live on mountain or valley; and at every christening, wedding, and burial, the bell shall sound, but only for us, the rich, and for the poor it shall not sound, because for them it is of no use."

And this wicked plan was executed. The complaints of the oppressed rose through the skies to Heaven, and in the autumn a great famine fell upon the city. The poor suffered dreadfully, whilst the rich locked up their treasures and store-rooms, and only gave the poor people, who came to beg for bread, insolent words, telling them that, after all, they were but a miserable lot, and the best thing they could do was to die in God's name, and go straight to Heaven. In this fearful dearth numbers died of absolute starvation.

Towards the end of the autumn, snow began to fall, and rose higher and higher, up to the windows up to the roofs, and then far above the roofs. In this extremity the rich people of Tannen-Eh' began to toll their bell for help, but its sound could scarcely penetrate through the thick walls of snow, and no help arrived, for down in the surrounding valley poor people alone were living, who had been cruelly treated and oppressed by the rich citizens

N

above.   So the snow fell thicker and thicker, just as long as it rained in the days of the Flood.

After this, Tannen-Eh' with its inhabitants had disappeared, but the tower of the church, together with the city, is still to be seen from an enormous distance, though deeply covered with everlasting ice.   The tower reaches like a silver needle to Heaven, from whence the Divine punishment had fallen.   This ice-covered needle-rock is the Oetz-thal-Ferner, and the city itself is now the "Oetzthal-Gletscher" (Oetzthal Glacier).

Even up to the present day the following song, illustrative of the fate of the city, is sung in the Tyrol :—

> " In the city of Tannen-Eh',
> Oh woe!   Oh woe !
> Fell a snow,
> Which never thaws again."*

> * " In der Stadt Tannen-Eh',
> Au weh !   Au weh !
> Fallt a Schnee,
> Und appert nimmameh."

THE DEVIL'S BRIDGE.

ALMOST every country possesses some legend of a "Devil's Bridge," and how the Evil One has been ultimately cheated by his own handiwork, and the Tyrol, which is alive with legends and superstitions, is not behind any other in this respect.

In the valley of Montafon, the bridge of the village broke down, or rather the swollen torrent carried it away; and as the parish was anxious to restore it as soon as possible, the villagers of course being unable to pass to and from Schruns, on the other side of the river, for all their daily wants, they applied to the village carpenter, and offered him a large sum of money if he would rebuild the bridge in three days' time. This puzzled the poor fellow beyond description; he had a large family and now his fortune would be made at once; but he saw the impossibility of finishing the work in so short a time, and therefore he begged one day for reflection.

Then he set to work to study all day, up to mid-

N 2

night, to find out how he could manage to do the work within the specified time; and as he could find out nothing, he thumped the table with his fist, and called out, "To the devil with it! I can find out nothing." In his anger and annoyance he was on the point of going to bed, when all at once a little man wearing a green hat entered the room, and asked, "Carpenter, wherefore so sad?" and then the carpenter told him all his troubles. The little fellow replied, "It is very easy to help you. I will build your bridge, and in three days it shall be finished, but only on the condition that the first soul out of your house who passes over the bridge shall be mine." On hearing this, the carpenter, who then knew with whom he had to do, shuddered with horror, though the large sum of money enticed him, and he thought to himself, "After all, I will cheat the devil," and so he agreed to the contract.

Three days afterwards the bridge was complete, and the devil stood in the middle, awaiting his prey. After having remained there for many days, the carpenter at last appeared himself, and at that sight the devil jumped with joy; but the carpenter was driving one of his goats, and as he approached the bridge, he pushed her on before him, and called out, " There you have the first soul out of my house," and the devil seized upon the goat. But, oh, grief and shame ! first disappointed, and then enraged, he dragged the poor goat so hard by her tail that it came out, and then off he flew, laughed at and mocked by all who saw him.

Since that time it is that goats have such short tails.

LAGO SANTO.

AMONG the high peaks which overhang the Cembra valley, lies a solitary mountain lake whose little outlet falls into the foaming Nevisbach. A small hut at the pointed end of the lake, and a deserted mine which stands close by, surrounded by large heaps of *débris*, give evidence to the former activity of the spot.

This dark lake is called " Lago Santo " (or Holy Lake).

Where it now stands there used to be a flourishing

village, whose inhabitants found in the neighbouring mines plenty of work and wealth; they were a
happy and contented race. A few miles off lay
King Laurin's crystal palace, and through the
constant communication with this good-hearted
mountain King, they became clever and fortunate
in all their undertakings. But, as time went on,
they grew haughty and independent; foreign miners
brought false doctrines into the parish, and as the
priest was either too weak or negligent to oppose
their wicked practices, in a few years the people
became entirely corrupted.

About that time a poor man arrived in the village
begging for alms, but all Christian charity had disappeared, and he was turned off from every door, even
from that of the wealthy priest. At the end of the
village there lived a poor widow woman with a
numerous family, who alone gave a piece of bread to
the mendicant, who told her in gratitude, "To-
night you will hear a fearful noise in the village;
however, you need not be frightened, but pray, and
for your life do not look out of the window."

After saying these words, the beggar disappeared, and when the family had retired to rest,

they were awakened at midnight by a terrible storm. The thunder was terrific, and the lightning streamed over the village, setting every building on fire; then the rain fell in torrents, as though the flood-gates of Heaven were opened. The poor widow was dreadfully terrified, and forgetting the command of the beggar, she looked out of the window, but at the same moment she received from an invisible hand such a blow in the face, that she fell senseless to the ground.

As on the following morning she came again to herself, the terrors of the night had disappeared, and the sun shone brilliantly down from Heaven. The widow opened the door of her little hut, and, to her great astonishment, found the whole country changed; the village had sunk beneath the earth, and a dark See was spread over the spot where it used to be; her little hut alone stood unhurt on the borders of the new-formed lake.

Sometimes it is possible to see to the bottom of the lake, where the avaricious priest paces slowly up and down, reading a book; he has neglected the souls which had been entrusted to his care, and therefore he has now to suffer penance.

THE ALBER.

THE Floitenthal, near the Ziller valley, is surrounded by such terrific mountains, chasms, and rocks, as are nowhere else to be seen ; the mountains of Floitenthurm and Teufelseck especially attract the attention of the traveller. The latter mountain is called "Teufelseck" (devil's corner), because it is said that at certain times the devil is seen descending from it, in the form of a huge fiery dragon. He then flies through the Bleiarzkar, a narrow hole in the rock, which leads through the Stilluppe into the Zillerthal. This hell-dragon is called the Alber, and whenever he appears, plague, famine, and war are the sure consequences.

It once happened that during a pitch-dark night, two men climbed the cherry-tree, which stands close to the Mission Cross of Algund, near the village of Meran. One of them, the tailor Hanser, was a most wicked man, an idle vagabond and debauchee; and just on that dreadful night he had made a bet with some of his worthless companions to fetch home cherries from the tree near the cross; but as he was a rank coward, he dare not go alone, and so he persuaded a good villager, the old Loaserer Sepp, to accompany him.

Sepp first ascended the tree, but could nowhere find any cherries, so he climbed higher and higher, almost to the very top, and he was very much astonished at not being able to discover the least sign of fruit, for he knew the tree to be loaded; as he climbed, he noticed a peculiar noise among the leaves, which disquieted him not a little. Hanser, in the meanwhile, had remained on a lower branch, where he found cherries by the hatful. At last Sepp shouted to him, " Hanser, can you find any?" to which Hanser replied, " Oh! yes, wherever I put my hand they hang in clusters." So Sepp descended to help his friend in gathering, but was unable to find one single cherry, while Hanser was filling his basket as fast as he could from the abundance which surrounded him.

Sepp began to feel very uncomfortable, and as he stood on the bough close to Hanser, he all at once saw the Alber fly by, lighting all around with the brilliancy of an electric fire. At this sight the tailor trembled so much that Sepp was obliged to hold him, to prevent him from falling, and said, " Has it already gone so far with you, Hanser, that the devil not only gives you his blessing, but lights you also to find all the cherries ? Then may God preserve you." He then shouted to the fiery Alber, " Hi there ! wait a little till I can find some cherries too." But the devil flew off with the speed of lightning.

Even now people admire the courage of the Loaserer Sepp, who dare do such a thing, and accompany the worthless tailor on such an errand; but as he was a good man, the Evil One had no power over him, and so he escaped the punishment, which otherwise would have befallen him.

THE OLD TOWN OF FLIES.

WHERE the village of Flies now stands, in the Upper-Inn valley, on a sunny slope of the right bank of the river, not far from the Pontlaz bridge, there used to be, in times gone by, a rich and magnificent city, with splendid houses, strong walls, and gigantic towers, surrounded by deep moats and ditches. But the inhabitants became proud and haughty, and practised all sorts of iniquities, devoid of any fear of Divine punishment. They were constantly quarrelling with the villagers of the surrounding hamlets, because they seized more and more of their ground, and robbed them wherever they could of their little cottages and farms.

One day they commenced felling a large forest, which belonged to some neighbouring farmers, who took their loss so much to heart that they nearly died of grief, for they had no chance of redress, as even the judges themselves were in terror of the cruel citizens. But there was still One Just Judge, who bends His head before no earthly power, and He brought a fearful punishment upon the guilty city. From a branch of the Venete Alps, a mountain fell upon the town, which it crushed, together with all its inhabitants, whilst the surrounding farms remained unhurt. These peasants then became proprietors of the new-formed ground above the city, upon which they have planted young forests and laid down grass, and the now standing village

of Flies has been built upon the tomb of the engulfed city.

— — —

THE SENDERSER-PUTZ.

In the Senderser valley, which winds up the mountain from Innsbruck, behind the villages of Axams,
Götzens, and Grinzens, upon the high Alps, stands
the Kemateneler Alm, also called Heach, upon
which the peasants of Kematen pasture about a
hundred cows.

On this Heach, so goes the legend, on the eves
of great *fête* days a gigantic Alm Ghost is to be
seen, who unchains the cows, and lets them run
upon the Alm, while with enormous speed and
strength he cleans the stables, and carries off the
litter in a wheel-barrow. He does this work with
so much rapidity that the mountain trembles; and
when the morning Angelus rings in the village, the
work is all finished, and the cows are again chained
up in their stalls. Of course, the frequent recur-
rence of this fact accustomed the people to it, and

they leave the Putz alone, as he never injures them,
but rather, on the contrary, renders them a great
service.

But when the good old cow-herd died, a new one
took his place, a man devoid in every way of either
religion or good feeling, who would not believe in
the apparition, and only laughed at all those who
affirmed its existence.   Soon afterwards, when he
heard with his own ears the noise made by the
busy Alm-Putz, he wished to sift the matter to the
bottom, and discover whether the Putz used a
supernatural wheelbarrow or the one appertaining
to his own worthy self; so, for this purpose, he tied
a bell to the vehicle in question.   The eve of the
next *fête* day the herdsman and some companions
heard the well-known sound of the bell which he
had attached to the barrow.   " Do you hear ? " said
the herdsman; "the Putz really uses my wheelbarrow,
so now he must only work for us."   And, in saying
so, he joked and sneered, in spite of the repeated
exhortations of the other men, who ran off in terror
at his oaths.

About a fortnight afterwards the cow-herd was
standing at midday before his hut, while his two

milkers were getting their dinner, when all at once
the gigantic ghost passed by, and the wicked man
shouted after him in derision, " Be not so proud,
sorcerer, but come and eat with us, since you have
worked so hard a whole night for us." The Putz
replied not one word, but striding towards the
herdsman, he regarded him so ferociously, that the
frightened man fled in terror into the hut, where
the Putz followed him. The milkers heard the
screams of their companion, but dare not go to his
rescue until the Putz had left the hut, and when
they found courage to enter it, they discovered the
wicked man lying on the floor, covered with fearful
wounds and bruises. They carried him down to
the village, where he died two days afterwards.

Since that time no one has ever dreamed of
interfering with the terrible Alm Ghost; the villagers leave him in peace to follow his favourite
mountain occupation.

THE DACE FISH OF THE GERLOS-SEE.

On the banks of the Krummbach, near the village of Gerlos, lie three mountain lakes, one of which swarms with millions of dace, of which, however, nobody in the whole valley dares to eat, because, it is said, they were originally put there by a Venediger-Manndl, and have the property of throwing all those who partake of them into a decline.

The legend says that a long time ago, a wicked peasant of that valley took it into his head to exterminate all his neighbours secretly and by degrees, so that he might eventually become the sole proprietor of the valley, and therefore he paid a heavy sum to a Venediger-Manndl to give him some poison fish to put into the lake. But his wicked plan ill repaid him, for he is now compelled to lie for ever at the bottom of the See, where the dace constantly feed upon his body, there being no other thing for them to eat in the whole lake; and, as fast as they eat, the body of the wicked plotter grows up again.

The belief in this dreadful legend is so firmly fixed in the minds of the inhabitants, that, even were they starving, they would rather die than touch one of the poison fish in the lake, and their indignation would be extreme did even any stranger try to take a fish out of the prohibited water.

THE VEDRETTA MARMOLATA.

NEAR the village of Buchenstein rises an enormous Ferner, or glacier, on the borders of which the neighbouring parishes, especially the farmers of Sottil, Sottinghäzza, and Roucat pasture large herds of cows. Only a small valley separates this spot from the village of Ornella, which, on account of its position, from November to February is devoid of every beam of sun. The aforesaid Ferner, which is above 11,000 feet high, is called the Vedretta Marmolata, and where now its icy fields extend there used once to be the most beautiful Alpine meadows and pasture grounds.

A peasant of Sottil on one Assumption Day had brought down from these meadows a cart-load of hay, and was about to ascend the mountain again for another, when his neighbours set upon him, and upbraided him for working on such a great *fête* day. But he laughed and jeered at them, saying, " What will Heaven care if even I make hay on a feast day ? " And, saying this, he set off up the mountain.

Just as he was on the point of loading his cart, he noticed that the dolomite rocks above began to assume most extraordinary forms, and even to move about from place to place ; dark mists began to rise, which at every moment became more and more dense, and then a heavy snow fell, which buried him and his cattle, and froze them into blocks.

On the following morning there was nothing to be seen but a glacier, and the peasants say, " There above are the cart and cattle, master and meadow, which have been changed into that Ferner."

O

THE TEUFELSPLATTE NEAR GALTHÜR.

AT the head of the valley of Patznau stands the Galthür, a lofty mountain, which rises also from the Hinder-Patznau, over 5000 feet above the level of the sea, at the junction of the valleys Montafon and Underengadein. Southwards from this mountain runs the Iammthal, or Iamm valley, about six miles long, and bordered by seven Alps; towards the Iamm-Ferner, stands a colossal ice peak, which stretches its frozen arms down towards the valleys of Patznau, Montafon, and Engadein.

In the Iammthal lie beautiful rich meadows, together with the Teufelsplatte, a rock which has been very much spoken of. An iron ring of 500 pounds is fastened into this rock, and it is said that the devil himself screwed it in its present place.

The legend goes that two peasants of Galthür had quarrelled several long years about a neighbouring meadow, and at last they agreed that the parish itself should decide to which of them the

meadow really belonged, for the vast parish meadows surrounded the spot in question. So it was
decided that the two peasants who disputed the
ownership of the meadow should throw a heavy
iron ring, and he who threw the ring furthest
should have the meadow, besides all the ground
over which he could pitch the ring to gain this
object, and the parish judge added, "If either of
you fail in throwing the ring over the meadow, its
boundaries shall remain wherever the ring shall fall,
and all that is lost shall be added to the parish
grounds; but also, wherever you can pitch the ring
into the parish grounds, so far it shall be yours."

Three days afterwards the trial took place. One
of the two competitors was a man who knew more
than other people; he was able to summon the
devil himself; and as with his assistance he hoped
to gain all the meadows in the valley, he made a
compact with the Evil One. On the day of the
trial all the villagers collected on the mountain,
where they found an iron ring quite ready, but of
500 pounds in weight. "Ha!" thought the parish
council, "all the better, for neither of them can

throw this ring one foot from the spot, and the whole meadow will be ours."

Now one of the combatants tried to throw the ring, but he could not even lift it from the ground. Then came the other, who, aided by the devil's own power, lifted the massive iron as easily as though it had been a finger-ring, and lightly tossed it over the valley, as far as the opposite rock, into which it became so deeply imbedded that only a very little is to be seen of the iron.

The parish councillors scratched their ears in astonishment, while the victorious peasant who had thus gained all the extensive and rich parish meadows, laughed and danced with joy. But on the other side, close against the rock, a terrible voice was heard laughing too : and that laughter was anything but of this world, for it was the dread demon himself who laughed.

Shortly afterwards the rich peasant became more and more dejected ; every one avoided him, and he avoided every one, and each succeeding year found him in a worse and worse state of mind. Once a terrible storm broke out during the night; black clouds collected above the magnificent farm, which

the peasant had built on his evilly-gained grounds,
and at last a thunderbolt struck the farm and set it
ablaze. When the neighbours ran to assist, they
saw a gigantic demon fly out of the smoking
flaming ruins, holding the rich peasant by the neck,
and dragging him, body and soul, to perdition.

On the following morning all the meadows lay
covered with stones and rocks, which during the
storm had rolled down from the surrounding mountains, and, as a memorial, the ring still remains in
the rock, which since that time has borne the name
of the Teufelsplatte.

FRAU HÜTT.

In the times of the giants, whom all Tyrolians
believe to have resided in the Tyrol during the life of
Noah, there lived high on the mountain, on whose
foot the capital of the Tyrol has since been built, a
giant Queen, whose name was Frau Hütt. Her
empire was composed of magnificent forests and
Alpine meadows, as beautiful, and even still more

beautiful than the far-famed Rose Garden of King Laurin, and her palace was so rich and magnificent that from every part of the surrounding valleys it looked like a tower of diamonds.

Frau Hütt had a son, whom she loved beyond all measure, and one day it happened that the giant boy went to pull up a pine-tree, for the purpose of making himself a walking-stick; but as the pine was standing on the borders of a deep mossy swamp, the ground gave way under his feet, and he fell, together with the tree, into the quagmire. His enormous strength fortunately helped him out of this unlooked-for bath, but he arrived home as black as a nigger, and his clothes infected the whole palace of his mother, who comforted her dear son, and ordered the servants to undress him, and clean his mud-covered body with crumbs of bread and cake. But the servants had scarcely commenced to execute this sinful command when a heavy thunderstorm came on and enveloped all in a dreadful darkness, while violent earthquakes shook the whole mountain.

The palace of Frau Hütt was shattered into one vast ruin, and then enormous mountains of rock and thundering avalanches began to fall, and in the space of a few hours all the paradisiacal Alp-land, which formed the empire of Frau Hütt was destroyed, the forests were swept away, the beautiful fields and uplands were covered with rocks and stones, and round about nothing was to be seen but a large desert, upon which not even one little piece of grass has ever grown since.

Frau Hütt was changed into a rock, and there she stands up to the present day, holding her petrified son in her arms, and thus she must remain until the end of the world.

THE TREASURE OF MAULTASCH.

ABOVE the route which leads from Meran to Botzen, not far from Terlan, are to be seen the ruins of the old castle of Maultasch, which was once the favourite residence of a Princess of the same name, and from her appears to have inherited this name, while another legend says the Princess derived her name from the castle.

There have been two different parts of this building, the principal one of which used to stand below in the valley to guard the route, and on that spot is still to be seen a hole in the rock, which leads into an underground passage, through which Margaretha Maultasch, the last proprietress of the castle, used to ascend to the upper part of it on the heights above, called Neuhaus.

In this passage is said to lie a hidden treasure, guarded by a fearful keeper, who is said to be the devil himself. Many people have tried to get at this treasure, but no one has ever succeeded; and the inhabitants of the surrounding country recount that, some years ago, two young peasants of Meran had resolved upon going to take the envied treasure. On their way there, they said to one another, "To-day the devil will never escape us." So they entered the passage, and began to repeat the incantations they had learnt by heart for the purpose, while throwing around them consecrated powders; but all at once a huge black dog rushed upon them, and they fled away, terrified to death, believing that the devil himself was at their heels; and, since that time, no one has ever again tried to discover the treasure of Maultasch.

THE NINE-PIN GAME OF MAR-GARETHA MAULTASCH.

In the ruins of the castle of Maultasch are also said to lie a set of golden nine-pins which appear above the ground and blossom every hundred years. This set of nine-pins belonged to Margaretha Maultasch, whose gamekeeper "Georg" stole and buried it when his mistress ceded the Tyrol to Austria, at Botzen, in 1363. Two days after he had buried it he was struck by an apoplectic fit and died, and nobody knew anything of the treasure. Since that time he is compelled in expiation of his crime to wander about in the castle in the form of a hideous ghost and guard the hidden treasure, and at midnight he sets up the nine-pins while sighing, and throws the golden ball against the large castle gate, which then flies open with a fearful noise. Then appear all the old counts of the Tyrol and Görz, some of them with crowns on their heads, followed by Margaretha Maultasch bearing an enormously massive necklace of pure gold, and the richest diamonds. They then begin to play, and the unhappy spirit of Georg is obliged to set up the nine-pins, but the ball always bounds against his feet so painfully that his cries very often are heard over Botzen and as far as Sigmundskron.

Only he who succeeds in digging up the treasure will be the means of redeeming Georg; but as it is most difficult to find the proper way and right moment, it has almost become an impossibility.

It is not long since that, in the favourable hour, an egg-woman went up the way which leads to the castle. The poor soul of Georg took the egg basket off her head, and put it down close to the tower on the very spot where the nine-pins lay buried. All at once there was nothing in the basket but ten black coals instead of eggs. "Throw your rosary quickly upon them," said the ghost; but unfortunately the woman had no rosary with her, and so the happy hour passed by again without being taken advantage of. The ten coals which were to be changed into the nine-pins and ball, became again ordinary eggs, and only in another hundred years will this fortunate hour return again.

The ghost climbed up the highest tower rock, crying and sighing his ordinary lamentations :—

> " He who will redeem me
>> From the power of the Evil One,
>> Must in the castle's grounds
>> Find nine-pins and ball
>> Which I stole from the Princess,
>> Which I hid from the Princess."*

THE DEVIL'S HOLE ON THE KUNTERSWEG.

THE ill-famed Kuntersweg is a narrow dangerous cart-way winding through a deep valley, overtopped

> * " Wer mich will erlösen
>> Von dem Bann des Bösen,
>> Muss in Schlosses Gründen
>> Neun Kegel und Kugel finden,
>> Die hab' ich der Fürstin gestohlen,
>> Die hab' ich der Fürstin verhohlen."

on both sides by huge and lofty mountains, and ending in the post route from Innsbruck to Botzen.

Soon after leaving this route and entering into the aforesaid track, the traveller arrives at a spot where the valley is more narrow than elsewhere, and there he beholds high above him a hole pierced through a bare rock which is known under the name of " Teufelsloch," or devil's hole. Beneath this hole are hanging several crucifixes and statues of saints in remembrance of the many accidents which have taken place on that spot—perhaps, also, as a consolation to the friends of the lost ones and an exhortation to prayer.

One day a carter drove by that spot, and as the weather happened to be very bad and the road swampy and soft from the long rain, the wheels of his cart stuck fast in the ground. It was in vain that he whipped his horses and tried all means in his power to get out of the mud. In this desperate position he summoned the devil to his assistance, using the most fearful oaths, and, lo! all at once there appeared before him a gentleman clad in rich green clothes, with high boots, and offered his services. The carter, who at first was almost terrified at this unexpected apparition, said at last, "Well, I accept your offer."

"But not for nothing," answered the stranger. "I shall help you only under the condition that you will give me a piece of your body." To which, after a short reflection, the carter agreed.

The green stranger had scarcely muttered a few incomprehensible words between his teeth when the cart moved by some invisible power from the spot, and when directly afterwards the carter was asked for the promised reward, he cut off a piece of his long finger nails and handed it over to his deliverer. Thus cheated, the devil full of wrath changed his form and, as a monstrous fiery lizard hissing with savage anger, and enveloped in sheets of lightning, and with roars of thunder, rushed through the bare rock above, so that all the mountains round about shook. And this hole has ever since been called the Teufelsloch.

It is no doubt for the purpose of expelling from this spot all diabolical effects, that in course of time those pious images have been set up at the foot of the rock; and most probably the road received from the hellish "Kunter," or apparition, which the carter met there, the name of "Kunters-weg."

THE SUNKEN CASTLE IN THE BIBURG-SEE.

ABOUT two miles above the village of Oetz in the Oetzthal, in the middle mountains which cross over the valley like a wall, stands the peak called "Biburgspitz," at the foot of which lies the little lake of "Biburg-See." On the spot where now the See lies, used to stand the magnificent castle of Biburg, which covered an immense expanse of ground, and it was in former times the scene of the greatest festivities, for a very beautiful and rich lady used to be its mistress; yet it is sad to relate that she was a very wicked woman and guilty of all sorts of crimes.

She had but one child, whom, like Frau Hütt, she spoiled in every point; she cleaned it, too, with new bread and cake crumbs, because they were softer than sponges. One day a venerable hermit who had been sent to warn the proprietress, arrived in the castle and paternally exhorted her to give up her evil ways; but in spite of him she carried on her wicked practices more than ever, so that the hermit went away in despair. He had scarcely left the castle when it sank, together with its mistress and her son, into the earth, and a calm See filled up its place.

But a short time afterwards the lake began to bubble and boil, and the guilty mistress of the castle rose out of it in the form of a fearful dragon, or "Lindwurm," which in its fury bit and tore at the banks of the See for the purpose of making an outlet for the water. This outlet forms the little river which runs through the fields belonging to the parishes of Oetz and Sauters; and the Tyrolians still say of little rivers that come out of the mountains: "Here a Lindwurm has bored its way through."

THE WITCHES' WALK ON THE KREUZJOCH.

NEAR the village of Mieders, in the Stubaythal, lies a little side valley, in which in dreary solitude stands a small wooden hut opposite to an old, half-ruinous farm-building. In this hut there lived, some fifty years ago, a wicked woman, called Töglas Moid, who was originally married to an honest peasant of the neighbourhood, who, however, died soon after through grief at the bad practices of his wife. After his death she led a yet worse life, and was in consequence everywhere dreaded as a witch; for she was known to have done, and to still do, endless harm among the cows. She had chosen five other women of her feather to be her companions and helpmates, and often the whole six of them set out from Mieders to the Telfes mountain, where at certain times they have been seen by the herdsmen carrying on their unholy Sabbath.

At last it seems that they went to such an

extent that they entered into a compact with the
Evil One, and then the destruction which they
caused in the surrounding country was so great
that the villagers were forced to apply for the aid
of the Church, according to whose decree they had
to appear before the tribunal, where the five companions of Töglas Moid confessed everything, and
from that time began to lead a new life; while she
who had led them on in all their wickedness became worse and worse every day, and carried on
her diabolical practices alone during yet another
five long years, until at last the measure of her
iniquities was full.

On the 24th of June, 1823, St. John the Baptist's
Day, a fearful thunderstorm broke over Mieders,
during which the mountains were splintered with
the lightning, and huge masses of rock fell down
from every direction into the valley.

On the following morning some peasants passing
by the hut of Töglas Moid, looked in to discover if
the witch was there; but she was nowhere to be
seen. But close by the Witches' Walk the most
fearful screams were heard, which so terrified both
man and beast that one of the herdsmen ran

down to the village for help; for the cows were panic-stricken and beyond their control. When the terrified herdsmen arrived with a crowd of villagers upon the witches' ground, they found her cut into pieces, which they collected and burnt upon a pile of brushwood; and during this operation such fearful noises were heard in the valley and on the surrounding mountains that every one was seized with fear and trembling.

The parish of Mieders erected in gratitude for the riddance of this witch a large stone cross upon the Witches' Walk, to which every year, on the 24th of June, a great procession takes place. This spot is called the "Kreuzjoch," or cross yoke, and from it a beautiful view is obtained of the valley villages of Telfes and Stubay, and of several magnificent glaciers.

THE TREASURES.

TREASURE! This ideal of earthly happiness constantly occupies the mind of the greatest part of the inhabitants of the Tyrol; and many are the men who, once wealthy and rich, now live on the alms of other people, on account of their passion for treasure-seeking. Over this hopeless infatuation they neglected their domestic occupation, and all at once, almost without knowing it, stood on the verge of beggary, at which they were just as much surprised as at having been unable to discover the envied object of their search.

There are treasures in all parts of the country, on the mountains, in the valleys, under rocks and trees, in the lakes, in the cellars, even beneath the hearths, and behind the walls. The ruins of once powerful strongholds generally conceal treasure in different forms, and there is not one ruin in the whole Tyrol that possesses not its treasure tradition.

Those treasures blossom from time to time, especially on the eve of St. John the Baptist's Day. Near Axams, in the middle mountains, above Innsbruck, on the spot called Zum Knappenloch, a treasure blossoms even in the broad daylight.

The blooming light of these treasures is described to be blue, like the flame of spirits of wine, or

green, like the light of glow-worms, and also yel-
lowish-green, like that of phosphorus.

The preceding legends already contain several
examples of these treasure-blossoms, and it would
be impossible to relate them all, for their number
would fill a volume.   But not very long ago a fact
took place on the post-route from Imst to Landeck,
close by the hamlet of Starkenbach, after which it
would be utterly impossible to make the inhabitants
of the surrounding country believe that the treasures
do not blossom.

On this spot several people had noticed, at different times, a green light, which lasted from two to
five minutes; but when they approached, it dissolved
into mist and disappeared.

Some men of Starkenbach happened to be at
work on the very same spot, on the 10th of October,
1854, under the supervision of the road-maker,
Tschoder, when one of the men, whose name is
Rundl, pulled up a piece of turf, and how joyfully
surprised was he when some two hundred silver
coins lay at his feet, most of them well-preserved
Roman coins of the times of the Emperors, and
bearing the inscriptions of Antonius Pius, Septimus

Severus, Marcus Aurelius, Geta, Caracalla, Maximi-
nus Augustus; others referred to the Empresses,
and bore the inscriptions of Faustina Augusta,
Julia Augusta. The inscriptions on the reverse of
the coins are almost every one of them different,
and relate to notable events of the Roman dynasty
in the country, thus, Marti Victori, Fortunæ Reduci,
Felicitas, Providentia, Venus Genetrix, and many
of them relate to Juno. The coins are all of the
same size, and five of them go to an ounce.

"Such treasures," declare the simple-minded
Tyrolians, "are lying in thousands all over the
country, if it were only possible to lay hands upon
them, as on those Roman coins."

WOLKENSTEIN.

In the Grödener-Thal lie dispersed in every direction about 135 farms, which form the parish of
Wolkenstein, also called Santa Maria, and above its
pretty little chapel, on the top of the peak of Sab-
biakopf, rise the ruins of the once famous strong-

hold of Wolkenstein, which is said to have been built in the time of the Romans by a pagan general, who through his wild and cruel behaviour became the scourge of the inhabitants of all the surrounding valleys.

One day a poor pilgrim went to the castle, asking for charity, but the general ill-treated him so cruelly that he died, and in his last agony the pilgrim cursed the castle, and invoked upon it immediate destruction.   Directly afterwards a huge mass of rock fell and buried it, together with its tyrannical lord, who was not less dreaded than the fearful Orco, whose abode lay in this country.

Some centuries later on, a wandering knight arrived in the neighbourhood, seeking treasures in the ruins of the castle; and it is generally believed that his search was successful, because before then he was very poor, and now he began to build a magnificent castle upon the old ruins, and called it also Wolkenstein.   Every future proprietor took the name of the castle, together with the title of Count, and up to the present day the family are a wealthy, powerful, and extended race.   One of their ancestors was the celebrated Minnesinger,

Oswald von Wolkenstein, who lived in the days of
" Frederick with the empty pocket."

Later on the castle was struck by lightning, and
one of the Counts built a new castle in the valley
below, and gave it the name of Fischburg; and the
old castle of Wolkenstein has since tumbled into
decay, but its magnificent and imposing ruins are
still to be seen.

THE GHOSTS OF THE CASTLE OF VÖLLENBERG.

Above the village of Götzens, on the route to
Arams, are to be seen the ruins of two towers, once
belonging to a castle of vast importance, and which
are called Völlenberg and Liebenberg. Two noble
races used formerly to reside in this castle, which
has quite disappeared, with the exception of the
towers above named; it is from these families that
the towers derived their names. The celebrated
Minnesinger Oswald von Wolkenstein, of whom we

have already spoken in the preceding legend, was for a long time prisoner at Völlenberg.

The legend goes that the spirits of the former inhabitants are still wandering about in those two towers; at certain times at midnight the ruins become alive, and lords and ladies, in long sweeping dresses, followed by liveried servants of the olden style, pass up and down the ruinous stone staircases. Their heads are empty skulls, and they sit down in the great castle hall, where they try in vain to drink out of large goblets; being, however, unable to taste the beautiful wine with which they are brimming over, they dash the goblets against the walls and smash them into fragments.

So it happens also with their unholy feast, which is laid out most temptingly before them on the tables; for as one of them approaches the dish upon which he has set his mind, it falls to the ground as dust and ashes. Then the wretched spirits endeavour to enjoy themselves with singing and dancing; but their bones rattle so terribly, and their companions are so frozen and stiff, that their song becomes a Miserere.

This is their punishment for all their former intemperance and evil-doings, and this terrible scene is only brought to a close by the ringing of the morning Angelus.

THE FRÄULEIN VON MARETSCH.

At midnight there is often to be seen in the old castle of Maretsch the spirit of a young lady, who wanders about, crying and wringing her hands, as though in the most terrible grief. Her long soft hair is blown wildly about by the wind, her beautiful face is deadly pale, and her eyes are fixed and staring. This is Fräulein von Maretsch, the only daughter of the Baron von Maretsch, and once noted as the most beautiful girl of the whole country.

Although scarcely sixteen years of age, she was passionately enamoured of the young and brave Baron von Treuenstein, who under Frederick the Red Beard, together with all the Tyrolian nobility, took part in his crusade, for the purpose of gaining

Q

the glory of knighthood in fighting against the infidels, which, according to the promise of the old Baron von Maretsch, should entitle him to his beautiful daughter for a wife.

Two years had already gone by since the hopeful young warrior had left the country, after having received the blessing of the old Baron, when one day a pilgrim from Palestine craved admission to the castle, and recounted the bloody battles of the Crusaders against the Saracens. In the course of his narrative he came to speak of the young Baron von Treuenstein, and said that he had conquered large districts, and at last had married the daughter of a rich Pacha, and thus made himself happy for ever.

On hearing this, Kunigunde turned deadly pale, and sank swooning to the ground; her attendants carried her senseless to her room, for the news of this dreadful infidelity had broken her heart.

Directly the young lady had left the room, the pilgrim sprang joyfully up, pressed the old Baron to his heart, threw away his pilgrim's garb, and in bright armour appeared before him as the Baron von Treuenstein, who had masked himself in this manner to prove the fidelity of his bride.   "Let us now quickly go to my dear Kunigunde," said he to the father, " to dispel the grief and pain which I have caused her; " and with high beating hearts they crossed the corridor which led into the young lady's room.

But the room was empty, and the window open; and as they looked down into the ditch which surrounded the castle, they saw the unfortunate girl lying smashed and blood-covered in the depth below. The untimely grief had caused her to lose her senses, and in this condition she sprang into the arms of death.

At that sight the young Baron became speechless.   He rushed away to the battle-field, and nobody ever heard of him again, while the poor old father died soon afterwards of grief; and since that time the spirit of the unhappy girl is condemned to wander about in the ruins of the ancient castle of Maretsch.

THE END.

PRINTED BY TAYLOR AND CO.,
LITTLE QUEEN STREET, LINCOLN'S INN FIELDS.